# A Sign

"What part of 'get out' didn't you understand?" In her five-inch-high spike sandals, Mandy Starr towered over the twerpy twosome, sizing them up as she stared them down. High school chickadees, she'd bet, who'd scored a parent-free zone for the summer. It had to be illegal for the training-bra set to be here—so they'd lied about their ages. A useful little factoid. No way were *they* getting the room she'd staked out—via Web photos—for herself.

The pale blonde in the designer flip-flops and hot pink tank top chirped, "I didn't know this room was reserved. There was no sign or anything."

Mandy shot her the bird. "How's this for a sign?"

You're invited to the next house party:

# LB (Laguna Beach)

## By Nola Thacker

# summer share

**Randi Reisfeld**

**Simon Pulse**
New York London Toronto Sydney

SIMON PULSE

An imprint of Simon & Schuster Children's Publishing Division

1230 Avenue of the Americas, New York, NY 10020

Text copyright © 2005 by Randi Reisfeld

All rights reserved, including the right of reproduction in whole or in part in any form.

SIMON PULSE and colophon are registered trademarks of Simon & Schuster, Inc.

Designed by Gregory Stadnyk

The text of this book was set in Stone Informal.

Manufactured in the United States of America

First Simon Pulse edition July 2005

10 9 8 7 6 5 4 3 2 1

Library of Congress Control Number 2005920240

ISBN 1-4169-0036-5

# summer share

CC

Cape Cod

# What Katie Did

"Darling, your ride is here," Katie's mom trilled. "Should I call for Carlos to help with the luggage?"

"I'm on it, Mother," Katie volleyed back in a light tone, calibrated to match her mom's. "Be right down." She had only to force her bulging suitcase closed, and wipe away that last bitter tear.

For someone so petite, she was strong: mentally and physically. Way stronger than she looked, and fierce when determined. Nothing sidelined Katie Charlesworth. Certainly not a trifle like a Tumi bag stuffed to triple its capacity. Least of all a telltale emotion.

Katie surveyed her bedroom. Had she overlooked anything? The light on her phone was blinking, indicating multiple new messages. She erased them without listening. For good measure, she loosened the phone jack, just enough to break the connection without looking unplugged. She double-deleted her e-mails, then changed her password. No one would ever guess her new one: Lilyhaterforever. With that, Katie closed the door and descended the stairs, "game face" on.

"Just one suitcase?" Vanessa Charlesworth asked. Her professionally plucked eyebrow did a practiced arch as Katie came into the living room to say good-bye. "Won't you be needing more clothes? For an entire summer on the Cape?"

Her mom's question didn't signal skepticism. In sixteen years (seventeen in August), Katie had never once given Vanessa a reason to doubt her. Not that Nessa would've noticed, anyway. The matriarch of their Boston brownstone floated through life on her happy bubble, never conceding it could burst. If only she knew the truth, thought Katie, fighting hard to sound normal over the lump in her throat. "Duh. I FedEx'd the rest of the luggage ahead." The lone truth in a sea of lies.

Vanessa raised a glass to her daughter—her morning toast was liquid. "That's your Charlesworth brain, always thinking."

The taxi driver leaned on the horn, not for the first time.

"Have the best summer *ever*, Mother, and kiss

Dad good-bye for me." Katie stood on her tiptoes to plant a kiss on Vanessa's papery cheek. "Be careful to use lots of strong sunscreen. You'll need it on the cruise of the Greek Islands and the tour of Bali."

To which Vanessa parried, "I will, sweetie. And you: Do not forget to buy Lily's aunt Sylvia a serious gift—something for the house, I'd think. And don't wait until the last minute. It was very generous of Sylvia and Henry to let you and Lily live at their home for the entire summer."

Katie nodded. "Already handled, Mom. I know exactly how to thank such gracious people." If an ounce of sarcasm escaped, it went unnoticed.

Pleased, Vanessa hit the "play" button in her clichéd (unfortunately, alcohol-addled) brain: "Breeding will always win out, a trait you and Lily share. I would have thought"—a tiny *tsk-tsk* in her voice—"she'd pick you up in the Lincoln Towncar. Why the taxi?"

Surprised that it had taken her mother that long to ask, Katie trotted out the prefab fib. "Her dad sent the Lincoln for an airport run, her mom's got the Esplanade, and one of her brothers commandeered the Jeep. By the time I get to her house"—Katie was afraid she'd spit if she said Lily's name out loud— "I'm sure one of the cars will be back. Not to worry, Mother, we'll arrive on Cape Cod in style."

Katie and Vanessa's exchanges were like a

badminton game, light and airy volleys, little puff-balls of superficial information bopping from one to the other. All very polite. No slamming, spiking, or sweating. Nothing weighty or substantive crossed into the other's personal space. Anything out of bounds stayed that way, was not retrieved. And no one ever argued the point.

Katie didn't see any reason to change the rules now.

The taxi driver, grizzled, grumpy, and BO-stinkified, made sure Katie knew she'd been charged for "all the waiting time."

Whatever, she thought, resisting the urge to hold her nose.

"Where to?" demanded the crabby cabby.

Katie gave him the address of the bus station. She shuddered. Not that she'd personally ever been there, but she imagined the Greyhound terminal a depressing, grimy place with dirty windows, sticky floors, and surly ticket agents (for some reason, she pictured them old and wrinkly, with stringy gray hair and bad teeth). As for the passengers? Desperate and ashamed that bus travel was their only option.

Today she was one of them.

She'd been to Cape Cod dozens of times—by plane, limo, or SUV. She hadn't even realized buses went there. As a kid, she'd spent summers in the tony town of Chatham, staying at posh resorts, or renting a mini-manse where her mother would entertain and her father, a Boston banker, would come up weekends.

Once Katie's friends were old enough to drive (or find someone with a license), her crowd would go for weekends, crashing at someone's parents' summer home. The girls, bikini waxed and pre-tanned, spent lazy days on the beach, barbecuing and (except for Katie, who abstained) downing prodigious amounts of alcohol. Some capped evenings off with a random and/or romantic hookup. It never "meant" anything. Always, there was loud music, raucous laughter, salty munchies, like-minded friends, and free-form fun. Oblivion. Lovely oblivion.

That was Katie, then. Past tense. (Future tense, if she could swing it.)

For now? The present was just plain tense.

"'Necessity is the mother of invention,'" Grandmother Charlesworth used to cliché.

Necessity had caused Katie to invent a mother of a plan back in May, when she discovered something Vanessa didn't even know yet: The plug was pulled on the family funds. The horrifying discovery had set Katie's plan in motion.

She needed to fake it, make everyone think this summer would be exactly like those old carefree Cape weekends, *three whole months worth!* Only this summer she'd be living in a luxury mansion with her best friend—without parental supervision!—shopping, sunning, and funning, sprinkled with large doses of worthy (read: wealthy) boytoys.

If nothing else, it would give her time and space to figure things out, and the chance to earn money of her own.

Her (ex) best friend Lily McCoy had rubbed mock tears from her eyes after Katie confided the real reason she needed to bolt Boston, fly under the radar, and what they'd be doing during those long, lazy summer days.

"Working?" Lily had sputtered, barely able to get the word out. The privileged daughter of State Senator Louis McCoy had been incredulous. "Kidding, right?"

"Kid*dies*," Katie corrected her. "We're going to be counselors at a day camp at the Luxor Resort. It'll be a goof!"

"And the punch line is?" Lily wondered aloud.

Katie laid out for her best friend what she'd privately dubbed "Plan A," for Awesome. As long as they were ensconced in Lily's aunt's deluxe five-bedroom mansion-with-pool, and showed up at trendy clubs at night, who'd be the wiser?

"But what about sleeping in?" Lily had asked, realizing daily drudgery eliminated noon wake-up calls.

"Weekends! We can sleep away Saturdays and Sundays." Katie tried to make it sound like that was a bonus.

"So let me get this straight," Lily said. "Monday through Friday, we'll babysit snotty brats for drudge wages, and then . . . weekends we'll sleep? Forgive me if I don't see the Awesomeness of your plan."

"Where's your sense of adventure?" Katie nudged her. "It'll be just like Paris and Nicole, only without reality TV cameras."

"Right," Lily had said skeptically. "And without being able to quit in mid-season."

That's when Katie played the guilt card. "*You* can quit, if you want. It's not *your* entire life that's being yanked from under you like some cheap rug. You're not about to suffer. . . ." She paused for maxi-effect. "But you can be the hero, helping your bff in her hour of need."

Laying the guilt-trip had worked. Eventually, Lily agreed to go along with the plan, help Katie keep up appearances, and earn coin. "Remember," Katie cajoled, knowing she was about to hit on Lily's (Achilles') heel, "I got us *day* jobs—every night we'll totally go clubbing and meeting guys." Lily McCoy was all about flings. Both a speed *and* serial dater, Lily's violet eyes were always out for a new conquest.

Just for security, Katie added the capper: "I'd do it for *you*."

She and Lily had long ago pledged allegiance to each other, and the fabu-lives they cultivated, deserved, and treasured—no matter what deep, dark secrets they had to keep and cover up for each other. So it'd been set. A done deal. With Lily's help, Katie could have the life she loved, while figuring out how to escape the one she'd be coming home to in September.

Until, just like that! Poof! It got undone. Plan A had died an instant and painful death when her now ex-best ex-friend Lily McCoy drove a stake through its vibrant little heart and pulled out.

Lily's weapon of choice? The backstab, the betrayal, the "Something Better Came Along, and too bad for you" bludgeon. And it was all for a *guy*.

Bluntly: She wasn't going with Katie to the Cape this summer. She wasn't going to be a counselor alongside Katie at Camp Luxor. And she wasn't going to be able to offer her aunt's luxury mansion, either. She was really sorry. (Right.) But for what it was worth, she, Lily McCoy, would totally keep Katie's secret. She'd make sure everyone believed Katie was summering on the Cape, kicking it with heirs, scions, and trust-fund trendoids, their usual crowd.

For anyone else, the betrayal (for that's exactly what it was) would have been a deadly blow.

But Katie Charlesworth wasn't, had never been,

anyone else. No one's victim, she—along with the mission the plan had been formulated for—was very much alive and kicking butt. It needed adjusting, was all.

Not for nothing was Katie called "The Kick" at Trinity High. She was the trendsetting, A-getting, acolyte-acquiring leader of her class. Katie's accomplishments were the stuff of popularity legend: captain of the tennis team, anchor of the debate team, she played offense on varsity soccer, pioneered the yearly clothes-for-the-homeless drive, and edited the junior class yearbook. Fashion-forward, Katherine Lacey Charlesworth was an authentic Boston blue blood without, so the myth went, a care in the world.

She was also hot. Not in that willowy Uma Thurman scary way—more "petite Reese Witherspoon as Elle Woods" adorable. Small, but far from ana', Katie's athleticism gave her curves a muscular tone. Her fine, platinum hair and kelly green eyes were offset by freckles, and a toothsome smile. Katie projected confidence and accessibility, the can-do charisma kid. She was hard not to like but easy to envy (a few wannabes, like Taylor Ambrose and Kiki Vartan, pretended they didn't).

She did have a pretty (damn—Katie only cursed parenthetically) perfect life. She worked hard at it too. No way was she losing it now.

No matter her father's heinous life-changing

screwup. No matter her mother's oblivion. No matter her once healthy bank accounts were now empty (which she wasn't supposed to know about). No matter Lily, the linchpin of her brilliant time-buying plan, had detonated the bomb too soon by backing out to stay in Boston with her latest tastycake. No matter Katie couldn't turn to any of her friends, or their parents' cushy Cape cribs—no one could ever know the truth—no matter, for the first time in her life, she'd have to go it alone.

Katie did what Katie does: She went to Plan B. Finding there was none, she created one. If it worked, the B would stand for Brilliant.

Technically, Katie wasn't old enough to get into a Cape Cod summer share house. But if she did, she would at least get to keep her job at the Luxor. Listing herself as eighteen, she went online and found the cheapest option still available. She'd bunk with strangers, stragglers like she who, for whatever reason, had waited until the last minute, when all the decent possibilities were long taken, and signed up for the last share house left. It was in downmarket (according to everyone, anyway) Hyannis, not Chatham. It had five bedrooms; Katie made the fifth housemate. A full share was $2,000, but she was able to split that in half by finding someone to share her room with.

Katie twisted her neck to look out the rear window of the taxi. Rows of stately brownstones off Boston's prominent Newberry Street stared back. Would the mailbox still say CHARLESWORTH when she returned? In the hot, smelly taxi, Katie shivered.

# Harper Hears a "Who Are You?"

Harper Jones plunked herself down on the rickety steps of the wood-shingled cottage at 345 Cranberry Lane. Placing her journal in her lap, she stuck her pen in her mouth and once again attempted to catch her thick, springy hair in a ponytail. The flimsy elastic holder was no match for the strong ocean wind, which insisted on blowing curly coils back in her face. For emphasis, it knocked her bike to the ground.

She'd been the first to arrive at the share house. The front door was locked—a credit card could've opened it—and a peek through the windows confirmed no one had moved in yet. She thought she might occupy her waiting time by writing, but her surroundings weren't exactly inspiring.

The clapboard house looked like the neglected barefoot child on the otherwise beachy-keen Cranberry Lane, less temporarily vacant as just plain abandoned. The front lawn was weedy and overgrown, a pile of local freebie newspapers lining the gravel driveway.

Yet Harper knew she was in the right place, this shabby shack she'd call refuge for the next three months. Katie Charlesworth's luggage—delivered just minutes ago, and for which she'd signed the FedEx slip—was proof of that. Five freakin' Vera Bradley suitcases jolted her into the realization that maybe—okay, probably—this hadn't been such a great idea. Too late now.

Harper would be rooming with Herself, the princess of the profligate and popular, queen of the quasi-wholesome and supremely superficial at Trinity High School. Why Katie had to resort to the desperate measure of posting a "want ad" for a roommate was a head-scratcher.

The first time they'd met—a week ago!—in the school library, Katie had scrunched her pert nose and tilted her head, genuinely curious: "So you really go here? And you've been here since sophomore year?"

Harper would've liked to pretend she didn't know Katie, either. But that'd be straining believability. At Trinity, Katie was known as "The Kick."

Half the school claimed her as a close personal friend, the other half wished they could. Harper didn't fit into either group. To her, Katie wasn't a person so much as a symbol—of everything Harper detested. Like: permanent perkiness, fashion slave, trust-fund Tinkerbell, teacher's pet, *and* valedictorian-bait. File under: "Good things come to those who need them least." On grades and test scores alone, Katie would probably be offered a free ride to college.

Spending the summer in Katie-twit-land was gonna blow.

But, Harper grudgingly admitted, it would blow less than a summer spent at home on Commonwealth Avenue, where she lived around the corner from the one person she could not bear, and was completely bound to run into.

Harper would not have survived bumping into Luke Clearwater. With or without his new girlfriend.

She shaded her eyes and surveyed. So this was Hyannis. Sounded like a shout-out to your rear end if you took a wrong turn at Pronunciation Junction. All she knew of HyANNis—not Hy-ANUS—was "Kennedy" and "compound." And that, only from some random TV sound bite. Harper didn't follow celebrities, political or showbiz, never read fan mags or tabloid rags. She just didn't care enough to bother.

And if Hyannis was where the rich and famous

came to play? Harper thought they could've done better.

New York, city of her birth and temperament, was the real deal—her real home, too. Always would be, no matter that three years ago she was uprooted, savagely ripped from her turf, her friends, everything that counted.

All because her mom, an actress-slash-activist, had gotten the part of "Susie Sunshine" on a Boston-based children's TV show. The steady gig translated into college tuition for Harper. Hence, the family—all two of them—had packed up and moved to "BAH-ston." Nothing good had happened since.

Certainly not her enrollment at the tootsy-snooty Trinity High School, a pricey private school for the talented and gifted. Except all you really needed to get in was money.

A fact that Harper's old lady refused to concede, insisting Trinity was the right place for her daughter. "You have a gift," Susan Allen kept reminding her. "It's time you accepted it."

Music. That was her gift, one she'd like to have returned.

Bored, Harper got up to stretch her legs. The house really was an eyesore, a pimple on an other-wise smooth ass of a beach town street. What royally pissed her off was the price! They were charging $10,000 for the summer! What kind of thieves, except those in the government, could get away with that kind of grand theft robbery?

Had to be its backyard. Every bit as ramshackle as the front, at least you got a fenced-in patio, two picnic tables, and a barbecue grill. Beyond was the beach. Walk out the gate, over the grassy dunes, and your toes were in the sand, the endless expanse of ocean big enough to swallow your troubles. Maybe.

The crunch of tires on the gravel driveway brought Harper back around front. A Volvo, boxy and staunch as a Republican, pulled up.

Out stepped J.Crew.

Or what Harper imagined the "real" Mr. Crew might look like: posture-perfect, square-jawed, sunglass-wearing, baseball-capped, decked out in polo shirt, faux-hunting khaki shorts, and Docksiders. In other words, straight-up and tight-assed.

"Ah, you beat me here," preppy-boy square-jaw said, taking off his shades and extending a large hand. "I'm Mitch Considine. Welcome."

Harper dusted off her cut-offs and introduced herself. Up close she noted crow's feet wrinkles around his eyes.

"I hope you haven't been waiting long. I was getting keys made." Mitch dangled a large ring jingling with keys. "Six—one apiece."

Harper nodded, unsure what she was supposed to say.

"So how'd you get here? Plane? Bus? Hitchhike?" Mitch asked genially, maneuvering one key off the ring and handing it to her.

Harper pointed to her racing bike, again prone on the ground.

"You biked from Boston?" He blinked, incredulously.

Harper stopped herself from laughing. There was not an ironic bone in J.Crew-clone's body. He got points for that. "Actually the bike's originally from New York, but I didn't bike from there, either. It moved with me to Boston a few years ago. Figured I might need it, so I took it on the ferry. I rode from the ferry here."

"Good deal." Mitch took the two steps to the door in one stride. "Try your key, make sure it works."

"Have you been inside?" Harper found herself anxious suddenly.

"Just long enough to dump my stuff," Mitch admitted.

Inside, the house was every bit as craptastic as it was out: musty, dusty, dank, and dark. Harper's eyes watered; Mitch sneezed. A foyer led into a room too small for the furniture squeezed in it: two sofas, a recliner, club chair, coffee tables, floor lamps, and TV sitting on the fireplace mantel.

"Behold the living room," Mitch announced. "The kitchen's that way"—he paused—"ah-choo!

"We've got three bedrooms on this floor, plus a bathroom," he continued. "Two more bedrooms and another bathroom are upstairs. There's a basement with a washer and dryer, room to park your bike. Ain't much, but it's all ours, all summer long."

"And it's beachfront property, so that's something," Harper added.

"Hey, we were lucky to get this at the last minute," Mitch agreed, removing the baseball cap and running his fingers through his short-cropped blond hair. "I didn't expect to be here this summer."

"Ditto."

Mitch mentioned other plans that had fallen through, his scramble to secure this house *and* find enough people to share it with. "I'm going to go pick up some cleaning supplies," he said. "Just so you know, all house expenses are shared. I'll spend only what we need to get this place livable. No worries, I've done this before." He winked and put his cap back on.

Confident and competent, as befitting J.Crew, Harper thought.

"We'll go over the house rules later, after we're all settled in," Mitch added, heading out the door. "I'll just go bring in your luggage."

Rules? There were rules? Harper hadn't considered that—or much of anything else in her haste to leave Boston. When Luke broke up with her, she assumed she'd go to New York, where she had friends, support. But when she saw the posting on Trinity's Web site, something crystallized. Better to spend the summer where no one knew her, and no questions would follow her.

Maybe not talking about him would lead to not thinking about him.

Her ex-hippie mom was cool with the arrangement, since a job at a day camp came along with Katie's offer. And Harper promised weekly cell phone contact. The only thing Susan Allen had given her shit about was not taking her guitar.

Mitch hauled the luggage in, which took two trips. "I suggest," he panted, "you snag the room with the biggest closet."

"It's not mine," Harper quickly clarified, "the luggage."

Mitch was confused. "Oh, I figured you sent it ahead." He checked the label. "Katie Charlesworth. That's your friend, right? Well, anyway, I'll leave it here and the two of you can deal." He slipped another key off the ring to leave for Katie.

"Hey, Mitch," Harper called as he headed out, "thanks. That was cool of you to drag it all in."

Our Lady of the Designer Luggage arrived soon after. She was sweaty, and obviously tired, but chipper. "Ugh! What they charge for taxis here is a sin,"

Katie complained as she trudged up the front steps, hauling yet another obscenely bulging suitcase. "I had the driver drop me off a few blocks away, when the meter reached double digits. I totally hiked the rest of the way."

Was Harper supposed to empathize? If Katie had blown her allowance, wouldn't Mumsy and Popsie back on Beacon Hill just send more? For that matter, why did Katie even need to work this summer, let alone spend time in a shitpile like this?

Ms. "I'm-The-Kick" *was* disappointed in the dwelling. Harper could tell by the almost-frown. "So," Katie said, "are we the first ones here?"

"Not exactly." Harper told her about Mitch and handed her the key.

Katie chuckled. "Sounds like we've got a House Witch already!"

"A what?"

"I was reading about share houses online. Apparently, someone has to be Large 'n' In Charge. That person gets to pay a smaller share of the rent. And ours is a *guy*, a Den Daddy. How sweet. Guys are much more maneuverable."

Harper was ready to retch—and bolt. She and Miss Know-It-All weren't going to last out the day, let alone the season. "You'll notice he schlepped all your stuff in," Harper dryly pointed out.

Katie surveyed. "Let's find the biggest bedroom."

It turned out to be one of the upstairs rooms. Its twin beds, covered in red, white, and blue nautically themed quilts, were set under Cape Cod–style dormered windows. A double closet faced the beds, perpendicular to a desk and swivel chair. Must be quite a comedown for Katie, Harper mused, again wondering how the privileged princess ended up here.

The girls hauled Harper's duffel and Katie's stuff up the stairs, sneezing, coughing, and sweating the entire time.

"Air! We need fresh air," Katie declared when they were done. Harper flipped on the ceiling fan as Katie threw the room's two windows open.

That's when the hurricane hit.

Fierce and unrelenting, it arrived wrapped in a miniskirt and whirled right smack into the room, shrieking, "What the hell are you doing here? This is MY room. Get out."

# Mandy's Got Big Ones
# (Hello, Plans!)

"What part of *get out* didn't you understand?" In her
five-inch-high spike sandals, Mandy Starr towered
over the twerpy twosome, sizing them up as she
stared them down. High school chickadees, she'd
bet, who'd scored a parent-free zone for the summer.
It had to be illegal for the training-bra set to be
here—so they'd lied about their ages. A useful little
factoid. No way were *they* getting the room she'd
staked out—via Web photos—for herself.

The pale blonde in the designer flip-flops and
hot pink tank top chirped, "I didn't know this room
was reserved. There was no sign or anything."

Mandy shot her the bird. "How's this for a sign?"

The other one, the coffee-complexioned Birken-
stock granola girl—"ethnically ambiguous," a

phrase Mandy had once heard—struck a hands-on-hips "bring it" pose. "We got here first."

Mandy thrust her own shapely hip out. "Which counts for a pile of shit. Scram, before I expose the both of you as underage."

Score! The flash of real fear in blondie's eyes told Mandy her instincts were sharp as ever. This one had grit, though. Wiping her hands on her Mui Mui capris, she extended her arm for a handshake. "Listen, we're going to be housemates, and this is off to a really negative start. I'm Katie, this is Harper. And you are—?"

"Pissed off."

Princess Paleface accepted defeat, and backed off. "We'll find another room, no harm, no foul."

Mandy wasn't certain the ebony one with the gray-blue peepers would go down so easily. What kind of a name was Harper, anyway? Upon further inspection, Mandy hazarded another guess about this pair. No way were they friends. The underage thing was only part of their deal. The rest? Runaways maybe?

The mulatto looked like she was ready for a fight, but the conflict never came. She growled, grabbed a couple of suitcases, and stomped out. The ones Katie couldn't carry—where did she think she was, the freakin' Hilton?—Mandy kicked out into the hallway.

● ● ●

Finally! She slammed the door and allowed herself a long, slow exhale. Mandy needed out of the too tight miniskirt and the pinchy sandals. She dropped backward onto one of the beds and decided to unpeel completely. Then, just for fun, she unpacked her black lace teddy, the expensive one, and slipped into it. The breeze from the ceiling fan tickled her bare skin. It felt good.

Mandy noted small cracks in the plaster, dust ribbons in the crevices, and made a mental note to tell Mitch to get with the Swiffer and make like Sally Housewife. That was his job, right? For that matter, the windows could use a good scrubbing, and the rug a thorough vacuuming.

Okay, so this dump wasn't Trump Palace. Straight up, to Mandy Starr, it might as well have been. She had a real good feeling about this place, like it was "Go," and she was about to roll the dice. She'd been ready for a long time.

The whole gig had come by chance. Some random girl had darted into Micky D's, ordered the low-carb sucker meal from her, and all of a sudden started squealing that she and Mandy used to know each other. "It's me, Bev—don't you remember?"

She blathered on. It was just to shut her up that Mandy took an unscheduled break (for which her cheap bastard boss would dock her, no doubt) to sit and listen to Beverly Considine, who used to live next door to her. Whatdya know, a few hundred blahdee, blah blah blahs later, one thing led to another—the other being this summer share thing that Bev's brother was organizing.

At first, Mandy had been all "what's in it for you?"—skeptical. Curiosity had led to her boss's computer, where she'd Googled "Hyannis." Possibilities popped up. Like resorts where showbiz types vacationed. Like marinas, where yachts delivered old-money types, and mansions, where politically connected bigwigs owned summer homes. Something else about Hyannis appealed to Mandy.

Kennedys. Talk about your money, status, and all that jazz. And weren't there a lot of them? *Star* magazine always had pictures of hale, hearty, fun-loving Kennedy hotties with coin and connections.

Thinking about the juicy months ahead energized her. She sprang off the bed, found a pop station on the radio, and began rearranging the room. Singing and shaking her booty along with "Hey Ya!" she dragged the nightstand away from the wall and pushed the twin beds together. That'd work. Mandy wasn't planning on too many nights alone in this room.

She unpacked the rest of her clothes. She'd only brought the barest of essentials, accent on the bare. The ratio of teddies to tops, cute undies to outerwear was 2 to 1. The one eyesore in her closet was the dumb-ass uniform that Duck Creek Catering had sent her in advance.

Not that Mandy was complaining. She'd been lucky to snare the job. The quick online search had brought up mainly day camp gigs. Right, like she wanted to wipe the asses of snot-nosed rich brats. There were "exciting opportunities" like the one she already had McDonald's, but she was tired of customers asking if she could—"heh, heh"—supersize it for them.

Just when she was about to tell Ms. Do-Gooder from the old days what she could do with her share house opening, up popped a position with some la-di-da caterer, whose clients ranged from the rich to the richer. Mandy was in no way qualified for the gig. She'd slipped her friend Theresa a fiver to invent a résumé and pose as a reference.

Ah, well, at least the uniform was black. She could say the top button had been torn off when she got it.

She was in the middle of creating a workspace for her makeup, accessories, and toiletries when her cell phone rang. She didn't recognize the number, and answered warily. "Hello?"

"Sarah?"

Oh. Her. "Wrong number—"

"Sarah, it's Bev. Don't hang up. I just want to see if you got to Hyannis okay, how the house is."

No one called her Sarah anymore. When would Beverly Considine get that memo?

"Can't hear you, bad cell reception," she lied. "I'll call you later." She turned the power off and headed down the short corridor to the tiny bathroom.

Mandy washed her face and checked the mirror. Despite her wan complexion and freckles, she looked older than her nineteen years, but damn, a whole lot better than the way she used to look. She'd take the "after" version over the "before" any day. It was good enough to net what she'd come for.

Barefoot, Mandy padded back to her room. Her hand was on the doorknob when she heard footsteps climbing the stairs. Male footsteps.

Mitch Considine, ever the good guy, lugging a very large, thin, rectangular box up the stairs.

"Mitchell! I wondered when the welcome wagon would come a-knocking."

At the sight of her in her black lace teddy, Mitch's jaw dropped. He nearly sent the package bouncing down the steps.

Mandy laughed. "You can put your eyes back in their sockets, mister. How 'bout a hug?"

He blushed and stammered, "I . . . hi . . . you look . . . wow."

"So I guess you majored in speech at that fancy Ivy League college, huh?" Mandy teased, pleased with his reaction to her. Not that ol' Mitch was any slouch in the looks department. He'd grown up hale and hunky, even if the word "prep" was tattooed on his forehead. If she hadn't known better, she might've put *him* on her hit list.

Mitch collected himself. "So, hey! Welcome. I'm glad this worked out. I came up to give you this." He motioned at the package.

She smiled. "My full-length mirror. Where I go, it goes. Maybe you can help me hang it in my room?" She posed suggestively—in a way she suspected might cause a boob to pop out the top of the teddy.

Flustered, Mitch thrust the mirror toward her. "Sure, later maybe. So listen, we're barbecuing at six, then all sitting down for a house meeting."

"Whoop-de-fuckin' do." Mandy twirled her finger in the air. "Can't wait."

"C'mon, Sarah. Don't be snide," Mitch warned.

"Hello! Sarah doesn't live here anymore. There is no Sarah. Think you can remember that?" To punctuate her point, Mandy thrust her extremely shapely leg out and let it brush against his.

"Sorry," he mumbled, trying not to look. "Just . . . well, put some clothes on before you come down. Mandy."

"Not to worry, Mitch," she whispered, leaning in to trace her finger down his chest. "I'll play nice with the other children."

She stood the mirror against the wall and unpacked the rest of her stuff. Her CD player, the food scale she brought everywhere, and her most cherished possession: her Scrapbook of Dreams. She stood it up on the night table. It was full of photos she'd clipped from magazines and newspapers—pictures of her quarry, her future. In addition to the *Star* mag Kennedy candids were shots of famous actors, producers, and directors, people she idolized and had made it her business to meet, people who, Web research had shown, often "summered" on the Cape.

People like: all the wealthy politicians, and their kin. Like John Kerry, and those ketchup scion sons. And snap, crackle, pop-a-doodle-do, some guy who produces the TV franchise *Law & Order* was making a movie on Martha's Vineyard. That was so close, she could almost swim there. And now that she looked so rockin' in her bikini, maybe she would!

Mandy was dreamily paging through her scrapbook, tracing make-believe hearts over Jude Law and Orlando Bloom, when her door burst open with such force, it banged against the wall. What the—? The wind? But . . . no! Oh-my-gawd-jesus-mary-and-joseph—"Heeelp!" she screamed and leaped for high ground. A creature! A thing! Like a bat outta hell, it flew in and skittered across her floor! It looked like the deformed baby of a goose and an elongated rat: long neck, light fur, slimy and slinky and low to the ground. The feral, alien creature squealed and squeaked!

Mandy jumped up and down as if her bed were a trampoline, and screamed as if her last horror pic audition depended on it. She didn't stop even when a flabalanche-fat girl appeared in her doorway, calling for the creature.

Mandy was freaked. She didn't know which grossed her out more, the fat girl or her stinky—and definitely off-limits—rodent-pet.

# Alefiya Explains It All

"It's a rat! Get it out of here!" The redhead with bodacious lung power went flying downstairs with only a flimsy bathrobe to cover her lace lingerie. What a drama queen, Alefiya thought with a chuckle.

Then, all through the barbecue that Mitch had so thoughtfully put together for their first night, Mandy had complained, whined, demanded, insisted relentlessly. "She brought a mutant rat with her! It invaded my room— it has germs. It stinks! Make her get rid of it, Mitch!"

Mitch tried to calm her down, but Mandy wasn't having it. She directed her ire at him, acting as if Alefiya wasn't even at the table with them.

"Clarence isn't a rat," Ali clarified, chowing

down on the potato salad. "He's a ferret. Actually, a black-footed ferret, which is almost extinct."

"Kill it then, and close the deal!" Mandy ramped up her carping. And her whining, adding several syllables to "Mi-I-I-I-itch!"

Alefiya, who told her housemates to call her Ali, did her best to explain: "I'm really sorry he frightened you." Mandy wouldn't even look at her. "He's just scared too. He hasn't settled in yet and—"

"Settle in? Settle IN? He's not settling anywhere!" Mandy banged her fist on the wooden picnic table. "He's a filthy rodent!"

"Not really," interjected Harper, the girl with the dimples, awesome black and blond curly hair, and skin darker than her own. "Ferrets were bred to kill rats. They're from the weasel family."

"Ha! I rest my case," declared Mandy, finally turning toward Alefiya, shooting her a look of pure revulsion.

Ali smiled and shrugged. If she got insulted every time someone looked askance at her, she'd be a millionaire by now. She wasn't stupid. She recognized knee-jerk prejudice when she saw it, but it didn't make her angry. At least, not in this case. Mandy, she calculated, was not a happy human being. No one who feels good about herself treats others like that. Maybe Ali would win her over, eventually, maybe not. No way would she play the hate game, or be bullied.

She doubted she'd get Mandy to accept Clarence as a sweet, curious, and loving pet. So she offered, "I'll keep Clarence in my room, away from you—is that all right?"

"No—"

"Fine." Mitch raised his palm like a Stop sign.

"Not fine—!"

"For now," Mitch said through gritted teeth, glaring at Mandy. "After dinner, when we're all here, we'll take a vote. That's how it's going to work, with this . . . um . . . issue, and everything else. Now, who wants another hot dog or burger?"

Ali jumped up. "I do! I'll help you."

In spite of mean-spirited Mandy, Alefiya was crazy-happy. Flipping hamburgers, turning hot dogs, just being here! Already Harper was her favorite. And that Katie! You just wanted to be around her, she radiated light. Mitch had to have the sweetest soul. The house itself oozed with charm. She loved the oddly shaped rooms, the cozy living room, her own slope-ceilinged bedroom.

The front lawn needed work, and here in the backyard the profusion of wildflowers and weeds could be plucked and replanted. Alefiya envisioned a garden with hydrangeas, impatiens, and maybe she could cajole some roses to survive. For Harper, a vegetarian, she could definitely do a vegetable garden. The poor kid had only eaten salad and bread

for dinner. She must be starving. "Do you like toma-
toes and cucumbers?" she asked Harper, "Those'll
come up fastest."

Harper looked confused, and when Ali
explained her idea, she said, "That's really cool, but
why would you want to do that? Isn't it a lot of
work?"

"Sure, if it'll buy your ferret-vote," snarled
Mandy, who'd overheard and misinterpreted.

Ali explained, "I'm all about gardening,
growing things. I'm working for a landscaper this
summer."

Katie came over and, noting Ali's gray and blue
college T-shirt, asked, "Do you go to Tufts University?"

"Botany major," Ali confirmed. "At least, that's
what I'm declaring. I have two more years to get my
parents to accept that."

Mandy mumbled, "If you have two more years,
better invest in a much larger T-shirt, since this one,
probably triple extra-large, is straining."

Katie looked stricken, and Harper looked like she
was about to whale on Mandy, but Ali laughed,
making a mental revise: Mandy hated her not for
being an Indian-American Hindu, but for being fat.
She said, "You're probably right, but that's okay. I'm
fine with the way I look. Maybe you'll learn to
accept yourself as you are too."

Mandy glowered. "So you not only look like Buddha, you even spiel that Zen crap. How perfect." She turned on her heel and stomped into the house.

Harper balled her fist. "She's toxic! She needs a lesson in courtesy, and if you don't want to, I'll teach her."

"Not the best strategy," Katie countered coolly. "We should back off. If you give people like her enough rope, she'll hang herself, without our help."

"So we should tiptoe around her like we did this morning and let her pop a fresh can of venom at everyone in her path? No way!" Harper contested.

"You—we—have nothing to gain by confronting her," Katie asserted. "I'm not saying we should let her step all over us, but we haven't been here one full day. Let's see how it plays out. Besides, I bet Mitch will be able to deal with her."

Steaming, Harper turned to Ali. "What do you think? Let her hang herself, or do it for her?"

Alefiya said thoughtfully, "I think the bitch has self-esteem issues."

# Mitch Makes the Rules—
# Like It or Not

Mitch intertwined his fingers and cracked his knuckles. Time for the formal meet and greet. Which he'd planned to dispense with over a casual barbecue. But Sarah's—ahem, *Mandy's*—tirade had pretty much canceled that, flat out. Besides, the entire group hadn't arrived. Joss Wanderman, the first to answer Mitch's ad, would obviously be last to show.

Mitch decided not to wait any longer. This was his third summer at a share house, and he knew the drill. He didn't mind being "rule boy." It was just like being the RA at his college dorm, a position he was well suited for. He liked managing, imposing order on chaos, being proactive, smoothing things out, and making the peace. He'd been doing it all his life!

He gathered them in the living room, planted

himself on the club chair, and took stock. Katie shared a couch with Ali; Harper, her feet tucked under her, had claimed the recliner (though she sat upright in it); Mandy sprawled out on the other couch.

These first days always felt like MTV's *The Real World*, except these housemates were not hand-picked by some producer to live together. This bunch was as random as random gets. As in: Unlike most summer share houses, whose members mostly knew one another, these were the scraps—like the people at a party who don't know anyone else. You bring them together hoping their one thing in common will be enough to forge a bond.

It was his first summer as a "scrap" too. In the past, he'd gone in on some cool house with his frat buddies from Harvard. This season was to have been different—only not like this. Mitch had planned to spend it in luxury, at his girlfriend's house—that is, Leonora's parents' palatial spread in Chatham, and without them there. Just thinking of her made his heart race.

But at the last minute, Lee's folks changed plans: They were spending the summer in Chatham after all. No friends, male or female: That was the rule.

Which had sent Mitch scrambling, ending up with this bunch. It was always a crapshoot, though, he told himself. You never knew how things would play out. Often the best of friends came out of the summer bruised and battered, not talking to each other. Maybe the scraps would prove a better mix.

He glanced at Mandy, already stinking up the room with her toenail polish. And at Harper, fire in her eyes.

Or not.

He chose the cute blonde, Katie Charlesworth, to introduce herself first. She had real charisma. He had a good feeling about her. And no, *not* just because she was obviously well bred and wealthy. He respected Katie for splitting her rent with the clearly less well off Harper Jones. Mainly, Mitch hoped to start this meeting on an up note, and Katie's smile was dazzling.

Katie did not disappoint. "I've lived in Boston all my life and, starting on Monday, I'll be working as a day camp counselor at the Luxor Resort. I'm pretty normal, really. No allergies or bad habits—that I know of! And the only thing I'm addicted to is orange juice!"

"What school do you go to?" Ali asked.

"University of Pennsylvania," Katie answered without pause.

"Yeah, right. I'll just bet you do, Doogie Howser," Mandy cut in.

"Rule number one," Mitch said in an effort to

nip the sniping in the bud. "If you have a problem with someone, come out and say it."

Mandy pouted. "She's a college student like I'm a—"

"Trash-mouthed ho?" challenged Harper, leaning forward her chair.

Mitch quelled the sick feeling in his stomach, although what Mandy said did give him pause. Was it possible she was right about the very young-looking Katie? At this point, it didn't matter. Who cared if she was totally underage? This *had* to work out. End of story.

"What exactly *is* your problem?" Harper shot daggers at Mandy. "You wanted the biggest room, you chased us out, you got it. Score one for the tr—"

Mitch started to interrupt, but Harper let it go. Folding her arms defensively, she said, "I'm a New Yorker, I'm a vegetarian, a Democrat, and"—she paused to stare down Mandy—"I go to NYU."

Mandy rolled her eyes, and blithely went on with her pedicure.

"One more thing," Harper declared. "I'm allergic to the stench of nail polish."

"Tough," Mandy retorted. At Mitch's glare, however, she closed the bottle. "I'm done, anyway."

Alefiya—Ali—went next, energetically describing her summer landscaping job. What was it about her that bothered him? Mitch had no qualms about

Katie—or Harper, for that matter. Mandy, he could handle. But this one? He wanted to like her. She was sweet, easygoing, good-natured. She'd been the first to offer help with dinner. Of course, on the flip side, she'd done such a messy job of it, he'd had to spend an extra half hour scraping the grill. A sign of general slovenliness? That could be problematic.

"Are you going to cook curry?" Mandy asked Ali, "'cause I can't stand the smell of that shit."

Mitch was poised to intervene, but Ali breezily laughed. "I can't stand it either. No worries."

Relaxed, Mitch mostly tuned out as Mandy presented—rather, invented—herself, listening only to be sure Harper didn't kill her.

His own well-rehearsed intro consisted of his roots in Boston, without naming neighborhoods; his current status as a senior at Harvard, without noting all the circumstances; and his summer gig teaching tennis at the Chelsea House in Chatham. He mentioned he'd be up early every morning for a daily run on the beach, if anyone cared to join him.

Mitch craned his neck to look out the front window. No one was approaching. He shrugged. "I wanted to go over the house rules with everyone, but it looks like Joss isn't going to make it. So, I'll just begin. Feel free to ask questions."

Unsurprisingly, Mandy had the first one. "How come you get to make the rules?"

He patiently explained *again* that he'd signed the lease, thereby securing the house, and had taken on the overall responsibility for it. In language Mandy understood, he said, "My ass is on the line here, that's why." Besides, he was the only one with share house experience.

He cleared his throat. "First, the obvious stuff. Drugs. It's your business, but it becomes everyone's problem if you do it in the house. So don't."

He purposely avoided looking in Harper's direction, figuring her—dangling earrings, peace sign, earth-girl—for a potential culprit, at least for weed. But she gave no sign of caring one way or the other. No one did.

So he went on. "Overnight guests. Again, your business. But too many people in the house invites chaos. We should set some limits—maybe one to a person, two or three per weekend?

This time, Harper snickered, staring at Mandy. "How many in the starting lineup of the Red Sox?"

Mandy took the bait. "At least I'll be having guests."

Harper stared at her stonily.

Mitch jumped in. "Anyway, rule number three: parties. Great fun, bad idea. No matter how much control you think you have, stuff gets trashed, the cops come; if there's drugs, we're all screwed. What it means, people, is we end up paying for restitution.

And I don't know about you, but I can't afford it. Any problems with anything so far?"

Katie contributed, "I agree. I've done lots of weekends, like at my friends' parents' homes. And it always becomes this mass event—somehow word gets out, and even though you might've invited, like, ten people, before you know it, one hundred are there. It gets to be a scene pretty quickly."

Mitch smiled at Katie. An ally. "Now, for the more mundane stuff. Food. You're responsible for buying your own, so label yours—it's really bad form to steal, or 'borrow,' someone else's."

He avoided sending a "this means you" message to Mandy.

"Now, money. There's a landline phone we can share, and even though you all have cell phones, we'll split the cost for local calls. Anyone calls out of the area, just keep track of it. I brought a laptop, which I can keep in the kitchen if you want. Wireless Internet, for whoever needs it. Anything any of us buys for the house is split six ways. I've already bought first aid stuff—you never know when you're gonna need 'em. I put everything in the downstairs bathroom. Also, the cleaning supplies—"

Mandy interjected, "Speaking of cleaning? You need to clean my room. The windows are filthy."

"Actually, Sare—Mandy," he corrected himself swiftly, "we're each responsible for our own room."

He'd raised her ire, though whether it was his answer or his near-slip of her real name, he couldn't be sure. He rushed on. "What your rooms look like is your own business, but the common areas, including this room, the bathrooms, and especially the kitchen, need to be kept clean. To keep it fair, we'll rotate those kinds of chores. The kitchen is the biggie. We don't want any kind of insect or rodent infestation."

"Speaking of!" Mandy swung her legs off the couch and sat up straight. "I say we get to the rodent issue now."

Alefiya blinked. "Clarence is a ferret."

Mandy's face twisted into a clenched fist. "No pets," she hissed.

Mitch sighed. "Usually, there *is* a no-pet understanding in share houses. But the truth is, I forgot to put that in the ad. . . ."

The look on the Indian girl's openly surprised face told him she was not going to volunteer to get rid of Clarence. "So, in fairness, I say we take a vote on whether the . . . ferret stays or not."

Without Joss, and Alefiya of course, the vote was split down the middle: Mitch had to side with Mandy on this one; Harper and Katie were a team. They compromised: Alefiya agreed to keep Clarence in her room—at all times.

"Until Joss gets here," Mandy had groused. "Then we'll take another vote."

Mitch remembered one more thing. "No duplicating of keys. Do not give anyone else the keys to the house. Zero tolerance."

"I don't like the rules," Mandy sniffed, miffed at having to live with a ferret.

Then *leave*, is what he normally would have said. But in view of the situation, he backed off. "Let's see what happens. If something really bothers you, we can put it to a vote."

"Oh, like we did tonight?" she groused again.

Which led to all of them talking at once—a chaotic overlapping of challenging one another, cajoling, squabbling, while Mitch pled for calm.

"What'd I miss?"

The screen door squeaked and, as if they'd rehearsed it, the five housemates turned toward it. Standing just inside the small foyer was a tall beanstalk of a guy with long, messy hair, ripped jeans, and a guitar slung over his shoulder.

Mitch found his voice first. "You must be Joss."

# Katie Knows Joss—But She Doesn't Know Why (She Also Knows More About Harper Than She Should)

"Welcome, counselors, to the Kids Club at the Luxor. I hope you're all ready for a wonderful summer—I know I am!" Eleanor McGeary, clipboard in hand, was exactly as Katie remembered her: robust, raisin-skinned, outdoorsy, and cheerful. As a kid, Katie had been a camper here while her parents, guests at the resort, were attending to their own priorities: supposedly, socializing and business. Which Katie now knew to be alcohol and fraud.

Ellie McG, as everyone called her, had been head counselor at the time. Now she ran the entire program. She remembered Katie and was beyond thrilled to hire her as a counselor and give her the assignment requested: the nine- to eleven-year-old girls—a group Katie liked best because they required the least amount of attention. In her (whatever, limited, experience) tweeners were all about cliques, clothes, and computers—instant-messaging their friends at home—not traditional counselor-led camp activities. Leaving Katie more time at the Luxor to pursue her agenda: meeting hot, rich guys—paying guests and their friends.

"Katie! So terrific to see you." Ellie came up and gave Katie a hug after she'd detailed the responsibilities to the group. "You've grown up beautifully, just as I knew you would."

"And look at you!" Katie, on Charlesworth autopilot, returned the compliment. "You haven't aged a day."

Ellie chuckled and wagged a finger at Katie. "You always did know exactly what to say." And Katie heard her mom trilling, "Breeding will win out." Her stomach turned.

Ellie turned her attention to Harper. "And you must be Lily. Welcome!"

Quickly, Katie cut in. "Actually, Ellie—here's the thing. She . . . Lily . . . couldn't make it. This huge family emergency came up at the last minute. So my good friend Harper Jones will be filling in. If it's all right." Katie prayed it would be. It had to be.

Eleanor was taken aback. "Oh. I had no idea! I'm surprised no one mentioned it before today."

Katie could practically hear Harper's echo, "So

am I!" Accompanied by a purposeful kick to her shin.

"It just happened over the weekend," Katie continued. "Lily's so devastated—she so wanted to be here this summer! Isn't it lucky that Harper's available? She's really great, and totally experienced. The kids will adore her."

"It's a little late," Eleanor pointed out. "Camp starts this afternoon and we don't even have an application, let alone any kind of background information—references, that sort of thing—on Harper, is it?"

It *was* late—exactly what Katie had been counting on. Too late for the camp to find someone else, making it easy for them to accept a substitute, Alt-Lily. Katie doubted Eleanor would quibble, let alone put the kibosh on it. She'd done her recon. Harper Jones had no skeletons in the closet, and, even better (and this was a dirty little secret she'd unearthed), Luxor Resort was sensitive to racial issues. They'd been accused of restricting golf memberships, and of profiling their staff. Putting the politically correct foot forward was important to them. Here was Harper, black, or least partly so. And here was a Charlesworth, vouching for her.

They'd hire her on the spot.

Harper hissed, "When exactly were you planning to tell me this? Before or after Camp 'Sucks-or' deemed me unfit to be a counselor?"

"No way they wouldn't take you," Katie assured her. "Look, I'm sorry I didn't say anything before. I had my reasons. Please trust me, okay? Anyway, our campers are waiting. I'll explain later."

With that, she broke into a smile and a trot, toward the gaggle of 'tween girls hanging out on the resort's tree-lined front lawn. The campers looked just as Katie imagined they would. The younger girls were ponytailed, cheerful, and chatty; the older ones, designer-bedecked, bored, sulky. The group replicated their counselors: one cheerful, the other Very Not. Harper had apparently settled for glaring at Katie the rest of the afternoon. It got irritating when Katie would make a suggestion like, "How about we call our group the Olympians?" and Harper would counter, "Rebel Grrlz is hipper." Or when Katie decided they should go over their daily schedule first, only to have Harper chime in, "Screw that. Let's get some ice cream first—my treat!"

Harper Jones was an odd duck, all right, Katie thought, watching the Rebels dive into DoveBars and Godiva sundaes at the Luxor Java Café. No wonder Katie hadn't known her at school. Harper defined fringe. Even though she was pretty, she dressed like a hippie, all faded denim, leather-strap sandals. And was there no end to her "statement" T-shirts, like REPUBLICANS FOR VOLDEMORT or CLUB SAND-WICHES, NOT SEALS?

Just like at school, she kept to herself here, too, preferring the beach and writing in her journal over anyone's company.

But all that was okay with Katie.

In the game of roommate roulette, she could have done much, much worse. What if Alefiya Sunjabi had been first to respond to Katie's ad? Katie had nothing against Ali personally—except for her relationship with cleanliness, which was casual at best. The girl was unkempt and unconcerned about what others thought of her. She left her smelly clothes draped over the sofas in the den, and Katie was constantly tossing her food remnants, also left all over the house, before they were covered in bugs.

Or Katie might've ended up sharing with someone like Mandy, whose itch to bitch, whine, and carp had not abated one iota. She strutted around half-dressed, like she was the queen sex bee of the house and everyone else, her wannabes. And the mouth on her! Truck driver talk (as Katie imagined it, since she personally had never met a truck driver) paled in comparison. Vanessa Charlesworth would've called Mandy low-class trailer trash. Richard Charlesworth would've just called her.

Why Mitch put up with Mandy was a mystery. Their den daddy was a find, a gem. Capable without being bossy, and unflappable, he handled Mandy firmly but fairly. Mitch had one more year at Harvard, where he was prelaw. Katie might have put him on her "to do" list—but the boy was taken (overtaken, you could say); he was a smitten kitten. Somehow, he managed to work "Leonora" into every conversation. Sweet.

Joss Wanderman was her big question mark. Because she knew him. Only not by that name. Nor by any other moniker she could think of at the moment. But there was something *very* (as opposed to vaguely) familiar about the lean, lanky late-comer. She'd figure it out, sooner or later.

Katie was focused on the "now." Time was her enemy, and it was a-wastin'.

Settling the group under a shady tree, she dialed up a big-sister persona. "Because you guys are cool, Harper and I have decided not to force some lame schedule of activities on you. We're the Rebels not for nothing! We'll rebel against the same old boring routine. Let's find out what you actually like to do, and plan our week around that. Agreed?"

Her answer was the rousing applause from her campers—even the older ones—and, unsurprisingly, a fierce glare from Harper. Katie hadn't consulted her about anything. She'd just economized, co-opted the whole Rebel thing, taking it one step further.

Later, Katie would confide that letting the girls do what they pleased (within reason—Katie was no anarchist) made for contented campers. Which translated into satisfied parents and bigger tips for the counselors. Surely Harper (just look at her!) could use the extra cash.

As anticipated, the Rebels self-divided into athletes and artists. Katie claimed the former—the swimmers, tennis players, soccer girls, and novice sailors—happily handing over the artsy, musical, computer geekettes and drama princesses to Harper.

After promising to take them for weekly shopping jaunts, Katie wound up with some very pumped Rebels. Excellent! Now, she was free to scour the boy-scape for candidates.

First stop: the Luxor swimming pool. A long, languid stretch of pristine chlorine, it was free-form, bracketed by a diving board and an excellent Jacuzzi. While her girls—Tiffany, Morgan, Jenna, Whitney, and Nicole—changed into their swimsuits, Katie donned her Hilfiger bikini and slipped into what Lily used to call her (f*** me) slides.

She wasn't out by the pool five minutes when she was approached. Awesome!

"Hi, I'm Mike, I've got the ten- to twelve-year-old boys." A pale, skinny guy wearing red Reebok swim trunks and a water-resistant watch motioned toward the diving board, where his group was waiting for their lesson. "Maybe our campers can get together for swim period?"

Translation: Maybe you and I can get together.

Katie shot him a friendly smile. "Thanks, but I don't think so. This is our first day, and we need to bond as a group. Maybe another day."

Translation: Not today, not this summer. Not you (no offense).

Just then, Katie caught sight of someone lounging on a chaise just outside the cabana. His legs were outstretched, a frosty glass was in hand, and an iPod rested in that flat space where his Boss boykini ended and his cobblestone abs began. Mmmm.

Quickly, Katie rustled up a cache of comfy chaise lounges for her campers. She expertly advised them on applying "lots of sunscreen, first, and always." While they were following directions, she sashayed over to Boss-boy. "Hey," she said innocently, bending over a little to catch his eye. "Would you happen to know where I can score some towels?"

On cue, he shot straight up and removed the earbuds. He had thick black curly hair and a killer smile.

Katie pointed in the vague direction of her group. "I need them for my . . . sisters, and their friends." Admitting lowly counselor status wasn't prudent.

He swiveled at the waist to point behind him to the towel cart. "Right there. They're big and bulky, though. If you need help carrying them, I wouldn't mind the distraction. I'm Brian, by the way."

Standing, Brian looked even better than lounging. He was perfectly proportioned, and Katie found the gentlemanly offer smooth. When he removed his sunglasses, a startling pair of blue eyes twinkled at her.

Oh, Katie needed help, all right.

By the end of day one, Brian Holloway, headed into his senior year at MIT, followed by employment in his family-owned Holloway Fund Management Group, wasn't even Katie's only candidate. Nate Graham was in the game too. During her group's tennis lessons, she'd wandered over toward the marina with a wire basket to see if she could round up the errant balls the girls had shot over the fence.

Nate, blond, cute, and clever, if a bit on the short side—and just arrived via personal yacht—had offered to help. Extraordinarily friendly, he'd even escorted her back to the courts, and given her suddenly tongue-tied giggly girls a few tips.

Again, the warm feeling of having done the right thing, against the Lily-pullout odds, filled her. Katie was having an A-plus day.

Ooops. Points off for Harper. Make that an A-minus.

The entire way home in the Lincoln Towncar—a freebie Katie had wrangled from the Luxor's courtesy driver—her (up to now clueless) co-conspiritor had been in her face, demanding to know why Katie hadn't bothered informing her she'd be assuming Lily's cast-off job. Had Katie just assumed Harper was desperate enough to go along with any plan? Or was it Katie's superiority complex, figuring, like, who *wouldn't* be honored to hang with her all summer? After all, she was Katie-The-Kick, wasn't she? All this, and so much more, Harper had shouted at her as the courtesy car sped along the highway.

Had Harper given her the chance to get a word in, Katie could've told her it was none of the above. Throughout the harangue, Katie kept her cool, knowing that no matter how furious the girl was, no way would she back out of their arrangement. Harper would stay the entire summer, be her co-counselor, pay half of the rent, and not be too nosy.

Katie's confidence was more than instinct. Katie had something on Harper. It was an unexpected find, an ironic and—when you thought about it— sickening coincidence.

At her first chance, when Harper went for a bike ride, Katie read through the girl's private journal. (Getting into other people's private papers, diaries, documents, and files, was a Katie specialty. That kind of intel came in very handy.)

But the Harper exposé? Juicy.

That boy Harper was pining over? The one she couldn't bear to be away from, even for an hour? Her erstwhile soul mate, the only one she'd ever loved, who had dumped her so suddenly, so violently, she'd felt (as described in the journal Katie read) "slashed open from chest bone to my belly, cut open and filleted, watching all the pieces of me gush out."

This boy, the reason Harper had fled Boston?

He wasn't coming back.

Nor was Katie's own erstwhile bff.

Luke Clearwater was Lily McCoy's better offer.

# Joss Knows Harper.
# Only He Doesn't Know Why.

Joss Wanderman stretched out on the sofa, tossed his guitar across his belly, and took a long pull of Budweiser. He leaned back, savoring the suds and the moment. The first quiet one he'd had since arriving here last weekend.

That it was well past 4 a.m. did not guarantee peace. Not in this house of harridans, as he privately called it. The recriminations, sarcastic one-ups—even the laughing, bedspring-rattling, and moaning, not to mention those infernal ferret noises—knew no curfews.

The main reason Joss had taken the late shift bartending gig—okay, the second reason—was to keep hours that kept him away from his housemates. Housemates! Had he ever used that word?

Yet, as he languidly ran his fingers over the six-string, he kinda dug the sound of it.

The idea of being in one place for a while was really what had appealed to him. He'd been on the road for the better part of the year, the past eight months a different city, different hotel every other day, or inside a tour bus. His lowly roadie status, even with a big-name rock act like Jimi Jones, meant he didn't get his own space. In hotels, he had a roommate. On the bus, up to six guys shared the two rows of triple bunks.

So when the tour ended and this came up, a three-month summer share gig, with a private room, he impulsively took it.

It was turning out that impulses were not his strong suit.

Since arriving last, he'd taken the only bedroom left. He didn't care that it was downstairs or that it lacked air-conditioning. Nor did the peeling wallpaper bother him, or even the fact that it didn't have its own bathroom. What bugged him were the paper-thin walls. And in the whole "one man's ceiling is another man's floor" category, his spanned both Alefiya's and Mandy's. The last thing Joss cared about was listening—and potentially being drawn in—to everyone else's drama.

Mitch had sought him out, the only other XY chromosome in the house. The do-good dude regaled

Joss with his Big Plans for Life with Leonora: the well-heeled WASP who offered old-money stability; status; long, winding driveways leading to sprawling homes; luxury cars; leisure tennis and golf games; 2.3 children with names like Taylor and Tucker.

Joss had no quarrel with Mitch—the cat was cool. Besides, it was easy to tune out the soliloquies.

It was impossible to not know what was going on with the girls on the other side of his bedroom wall. Katie and Harper—jailbait, like so many groupies he'd seen. In his habit, Joss had renamed them: Smilin' Suzie Q and Angry Young Babe. How'd this deuce end up roommates, anyway?

SSQ, so clearly a pampered princess from the not-so-faraway land of the Boston blue bloods, was such a phony! She wanted everyone to think of her as radiant, cool, collected—like she wasn't repulsed by the shoddy share house and her random roommates.

It was the condescending tone she used with Mandy when "complimenting" one of her trashier outfits, or "supporting" Mandy's getting-into-show-biz goal. If SSQ believed she was hiding her "I'm so above all of you" attitude, she was mistaken. Joss saw the way her nose scrunched whenever she tossed one of Alefiya's half-eaten overripe plums or sweaty peaches left in the den; the disapproving eyes she cast on the carefree chick when she brought

home a stray. Ali's strays often came with gifts—
cannabis, for sure; maybe other substances—and
stayed the night.

Just to fuck with SSQ, Joss was sure, AYB purposely got closer to Alefiya. He liked that about her.

Not that Joss took sides. It was his misfortune to
be able to see things from both points of view. He
could make all the private fun of Katie he wanted,
but he felt her pain, man. He knew the effort it took
to put on a carefree face, to pretend everything was
peachy keen, all the time. Why she was here, in this
pit stop, let alone sharing a bedroom, was a head-
scratcher, but he hoisted his beer bottle in a silent
salute. He wished Katie well.

Deciphering Harper wasn't so easy. When she
wasn't messing with Katie, she was making herself
scarce. She wasn't here for the company, and she
sure wasn't here for a hookup. Girls gave off vibes—
he could always tell what they wanted.

He didn't know where the fury and subversive
behavior came from. Not that teenagers, and he
was sure she was one, needed a reason to be pissed
off. But there was something about her that
intrigued him. "Something," as the Beatles
famously said, "in the way she moves," attracted
him, was *familiar* to him. Like the way she stuck her
lower lip out when she was pondering something;
the way her eyes flashed when arguing with Katie;

the unexpected dimples on those rare occasions she smiled; and those coltish, bordering on ungainly, strides even when her chin was stuck out defiantly.

Who did that remind him of? Between the beer buzz and the quiet, he settled in to ponder. His reverie was rudely interrupted by the slam of the screen door. He bolted up, saw her before she saw him.

Took in the angry slash of her mouth, the flashing eyes furiously blinking back the tears, and the deliberate stomping of her heels. Mandy. Their very own menace to society was headed toward the steps.

Soundlessly, Joss lowered himself, hoping the high back of the couch would conceal him. If he could have, he would've rolled under it, disappeared until the coast was clear. No luck.

It must've been out of the corner of her mascara-smudged eye that she'd seen a flash. He heard her pivot on her clicking heels, away from the steps. Toward the sofa. There was no escape.

Before he could decide whether to acknowledge her or pretend to be asleep, she was staring down at him. Then she was bending over the back of the couch, making sure he got a load of her cleavage popping out of her waitress uniform. What, did she think he'd never seen boobs before?

"Whatcha' doing up?" she said, righting herself.

Joss propped himself up on his elbows. "Just got in from work. Looks like you worked the late shift too?"

He didn't really want to know the tawdry details of why Mandy looked like a train wreck, but he couldn't ignore her.

She sniffed and ran her fingers through her thick red hair. "Yeah, the late shift. You could say that." She nodded at his beer. "Any more in the fridge?"

"It's labeled," he warned, knowing there were a few bottles left with Mitch's name on them.

"Cool," she said.

She flipped direction again, heading toward the kitchen. Now's the moment he could feign exhaustion, or simply slink away. He didn't. Not then, or during the ten minutes it took her to go upstairs and "freshen up" either.

When Mandy returned, she was barefoot and clad in a silky robe. She settled on the sofa. His sofa. She sat on the far end, to be sure, but crossed her legs so the robe would part, revealing shapely thighs. As if he didn't get the memo, she licked her lips suggestively after her first chug of beer.

Joss sighed. Could she be any more obvious? He hoped he wasn't, acknowledging that, sometimes, his body had a mind of its own.

"So Mitch says you're, like, a drifter," Mandy said after a while. "True?"

He considered, plucked a string on his guitar. "I've been traveling a lot lately." Joss had deliberately stayed away from discussions of his background. It wasn't hard to do. Most people were more interested in talking about themselves, if you asked. Of Mandy, he asked what had happened tonight, why she looked so upset when she got in.

She tried to sound casual, but her eyes darkened. "Let's just say the night was disappointing."

"You're working for some catering company, right? Is that cool?"

Now she brightened. "Duck Creek. It's very exclusive."

"Is it, now?" Joss feigned interest.

"They don't advertise, they only take recommendations. That means really stinking rich people," she confided. "You wouldn't believe the mansions these people live in—and, for some of them, they're only summer homes! And the decor!" Or, as Mandy pronounced it, "DAY-core." They have real antiques, and big paintings on the walls, and chandeliers. Like you see in movies, only real."

Joss chastised himself. For Mandy, this was real. And hadn't he said he wanted to break out of his gilded cage and meet real people? He coaxed, "So your job is to butler food around, pass the hors d'oeuvres?"

"Well, that's what I'm doing now. But I'm not really a waitress."

"You're working toward another career?" he guessed, working at keeping the jadedness out of his voice.

Mandy stared at him. All he saw were her lips. Joss felt his stomach do a flip-flop. When she got up to get more beers for the two of them, she passed in front of him, the hem of her robe lightly brushing his leg. Joss calculated Mitch's beer was all gone now. He opened it, anyway. Mandy was about to tell him something. Please don't let it be, "I want to be an actress/rock star/model. This job is temporary, until I get my big break."

"I'm going to be an actress-model. And I only took this job . . ."

Joss swallowed, his eyes downcast. She'd finished explaining, was waiting for a response. He knew exactly what he should say: "Listen, I know those people, Mandy, and trust me, they're not going to help you. No matter what they say, or promise, this is not the way to an acting career. To them, you're a dime a dozen, a girl they'll string along, pretend to be interested in. Until they get what they want. Then they'll toss you away, like garbage." Only what Joss heard himself say was, "That's"—he took another swig of beer—"interesting."

"You bet it is," Mandy said. "I've been working a long time for this opportunity. Getting myself in shape, and stuff. Now's my time."

"So what happened tonight? Did someone stiff you?"

Mandy found that funny. Of course, she'd had a

few beers by then. "You could put it that way."

"What other way could you put it?"

She shrugged. "Miscommunication. I thought I was saying one thing. This producer—he's about to start a big movie—thought I was saying something else. His wife had another interpretation."

Okay, she'd given him the opening to gently tell her that she might want to rethink this—her plan could only lead to disaster. But all that came out was, "I'm sorry."

She nodded toward the guitar. "Are you a musician?"

"You could put it that way." This was verbal foreplay. He hated himself for doing it. So he tried to repair, by talking. "I've actually been on the road with this rock band—I'm not in it," he clarified at her real interest. "I do some fill-in licks, but mostly I'm a roadie. You know, carry the equipment, stuff like that."

"What rock band?"

"Jimi Jones."

Her eyes widened. "No shit! He's, like, a guitar legend. Would you play something for me?"

Joss's heart was thumping. "I don't want to wake anyone," he whispered hoarsely.

"So play quietly. I'll come closer." As she did, the ribbon tying her robe fell loose. And Joss couldn't refuse either of her requests.

# And on the Weekend, We Play. But Not Before We Do Our Chores. And Try Not to Air Too Much Dirty Laundry.

### Mitch Feels Flush. This Is a Good Thing!

Mitch arose extra early on Saturday morning, feeling pumped, like Johnny Damon on a streak. He went over his mental to-do list during his run along the shoreline. He'd decreed today as the first official cleanup day: They'd been in the house just over a week, and it was time. To that end, he'd slipped copies of the who-does-what housework "wheel" under everyone's door last night.

Experience of summers past had taught him that a communal breakfast would be a nice touch. After his run, he drove into town to get a dozen bagels, cream cheese, lox, freshly baked

Cinnabons, and flavored coffee. His treat.

In spite of a few first-week flare-ups, the share house seemed to be running smoothly. Issues were part of the game, what with half-a-dozen different personalities crammed into one small cottage. Mitch was sure they'd iron themselves out, given a few more days. Mr. Optimism, that's how he felt these days. And why not?

The tennis-playing patrons at Chelsea House in Chatham loved him. Already, week one, he'd snared a cache of new clients who'd signed up for the entire summer. Regulars guaranteed him a nice salary and, if he could keep his A-game going, hefty gratuities by summer's end.

The diamond ring he'd been secretly saving for would be his—Leonora's—ahead of schedule. They could be engaged by Labor Day.

Mitch had been bummed at the last-minute boot from Leonora's house, but now saw the upside. If the marriage proposal was to be a magical surprise, not living together was actually better. He kept his ever-expanding cash-stash in his room: An arrangement had already been secured with a jeweler to get a better-grade diamond if he paid in cash. This way, Leonora couldn't accidentally discover how much money he had spent and start asking questions.

So far, Mitch and Leonora had only seen each

other once, briefly, in the week he'd been there, but they'd talked every night. Mitch had the tiniest sense that something was wrong, but Lee hadn't responded when he'd asked. Whatever. He'd find out tonight. They were having dinner at Le Jardin, and face-to-face she never could keep a secret from him.

### Harper Sees Red. This Is Not a Good Thing.

It was the aroma of the hazelnut and vanilla coffee Mitch had brewed that brought Harper to the kitchen counter first. No one did bagels like New York, but she had to admit, chomping heartily into the pumpernickel raisin, this came close. And the coffee wasn't from evil corporate monster Starbucks! Mitch got kudos for that, and for supplying the breakfast treats.

Cheerily, his square face aglow, he asked, "So, how goes it at day camp?"

Harper inhaled her coffee . . . mmmm . . . and shrugged. "It'll be fine. The campers are spoiled brats, and Katie caters to their every materialistic whim. . . ." She paused. "You didn't go there as a kid, did you?"

Mitch laughed. "Hardly. Thank you for thinking that, though. Very flattering."

Harper cocked her head. "Why?"

Mitch was guileless. "Why am I flattered? To look like I could've spent my summers at the Luxor, as a rich guest? Who wouldn't be flattered?"

He wasn't being sarcastic. He really thought that was a good thing. So, he hadn't been a prep all his life. Although . . . Harper took in his polo shirt, collar turned up, and belted Hilfiger shorts. He sure was one now. Mitch really did believe everyone aspires, or should, to the genteel life. Harper could've argued the point. But another sip of the glorious coffee, and the soft, still warm, inner-tube belly of the bagel, mellowed her. In spite of his superficial values, Mitch was a good guy.

"You're a freakin' buzz kill, Mitch, you know that?"

Harper spun around on her stool.

And there was Mandy, bedecked in one of her bawdy boudoir ensembles, waving a copy of the chore wheel in Mitch's face. "I'm not cleaning the stinking crapper."

Harper had to clamp her palm over her mouth to keep from laughing. Could there be two people more opposite than Mitch and Mandy? And yet, there was this in common: They said exactly what was on their minds.

Mitch rounded the counter and put an outstretched hand on Mandy's shoulder. "No choice.

Everyone's gotta do them. It's not a big deal."

"Yeah it is—the upstairs bathroom stinks! From her I-don't-know-what, her curry smell!"

Harper nearly choked. Mandy had spoken her mind, all right. Her racist mind. Harper bolted off the kitchen stool. But Mitch was all over it. He tightened his grip on her shoulder. "I'll pretend you didn't say that. I'll get some deodorizing disinfectant. You can spray it first, and then do the cleaning."

"I don't care if you fill the fucking room with fucking Renuzit," Mandy cursed. "That smell won't come out. And I'm not submitting myself to it. Besides," she sniffed, "it's bad enough I have to live in the same house with her."

Mitch growled, "You don't like her? You're an actress. *Act* like you do!"

"Good morning!" Alefiya sailed into the kitchen, her sunny voice matching her ear-to-ear grin. "Smells so good in here! What is it? Coffee? Oh, and Cinnabons, too! What's the occasion?"

Silence. Ali looked from face to face. "What's wrong? You guys are so grim. Did we lose our lease or something?"

Harper jumped in: "Mandy thinks it's beneath her to clean the bathroom. But that's how this week's wheel of misfortune spins."

Ali looked puzzled. "That's the problem? Our

bathroom upstairs? Forget it. I'll do it."

Mitch eyed her warily. "You'll switch jobs with her this time, you mean?"

Helping herself to a Cinnabon, Ali answered, "I'll just do it every week. I don't care."

Harper began to boil. She wanted to shake some sense into Ali, to tell her what a cheap little racist Mandy was. And look at her. Mandy wasn't even grateful! She just planted herself at the table and began butchering her bagel, tearing out the bready (caloric, and best) part.

"Ummm . . . delicious!" Alefiya managed that with her mouth full as she plopped down in the chair next to Mandy—who pulled hers away ever so slightly.

Mitch scratched his head. "You were supposed to do yard work, Ali. Do you want to hold off on that today?"

Licking the gooey sugary topping from her fingers, she said, "No, that's okay. I have do the vegetable garden, anyway, so I'll do it all at the same time. It's all good."

Harper forced herself to chill. "It is so cool of you to do that garden. I'll help if I can." The garden was for her benefit. Ali's bid to fill the fridge with organic, homegrown veggies. The girl was just genuinely good-hearted. Harper wished her housemate could be more discriminating.

Katie waltzed into the kitchen. She looked like she'd been at a tween slumber party, in her drawstring Juicy Couture sweat bottoms and glittery pink tank top. Only, flip it: This was not sunny-side-up Katie. This Katie nodded curtly and made for the fridge. Flinging open the door, she whined, "Oh, sugar! Where's there orange juice? I just bought half a gallon two days ago."

Oh, *sugar?* Harper guffawed, nearly sending coffee out her nostrils. Who talks like that?

"And good morning to you," Mitch said genially. "How 'bout a bagel?"

Katie frowned. "Sorry. This stuff looks appetizing, I just like to start my mornings with O.J. And I was positive I had plenty left. She directed her comment at Ali. "I happened to notice you having a glass yesterday. Any chance that might've been mine?"

Ali shrugged. "To be honest, I'm not sure."

Katie's jaw clenched, but she managed to sound reasonable. "If you'd finished someone else's juice, you don't think you'd notice?"

Ali threw her hands up, surrendering. "I could be guilty. Sorry."

Harper couldn't resist the urge to butt in. "How do you know *she* finished it? Maybe it was one of us."

Katie colored. "It wasn't you. You only drink organic. It wasn't Mandy, who's off sugar. Mitch has principles, and Joss sleeps through breakfast. If it wasn't Alefiya, it was one of her overnight guests."

Ali conceded. "Okay, sure, it was probably me. My bad. I didn't realize how much it meant to you."

"Well, now that you know," Katie said a tad too brightly, "kindly stick to your own stuff from now on."

"Oooh, see Katie being cross," Harper taunted. "See Katie being disapproving. Why is Katie really so cross?"

Katie scowled at Harper.

No one noticed Joss saunter in. Clad in shorts, wife-beater tank top, and sandals, he was a taller, buffer Ryan Atwood pouring himself coffee. Katie cut her eyes at him and sniffed, "I'm just a little tired. I got in late from a date."

"Miss Popularity strikes again," said Harper.

"Whatever. I've got a living room to dust and carpet fragments to vacuum. Toodles, y'all."

### Katie Sees Joss Blush.

Katie wasn't hungry. Her throat was filled with bile. Swallowing it was all she could handle. She didn't know who got on her nerves more: Alefiya or Harper. Not that Mandy, or whatever her real name was, was any great shakes either. She could barely believe she was stuck in this hovel with *any* of them.

Joss leaned against the fridge. "You were at The Naked Oyster last night, right? With a dark-haired guy? At the corner table, facing the bar?"

This caught Katie by surprise. "You were there?"

"I work there," Joss said, "bartending."

"Oh, duh." Sweetly, Katie smacked her palm against her forehead. "I so knew that! I can't believe I didn't say hi."

"Well, you looked kinda busy. Pretty . . . involved."

Katie grinned. Since meeting Brian and Nate, she'd been out with each. They'd hit select bars in Hyannisport, plus (of course) the Cracked Claw in Chatham. She routinely ran into people who counted (translation: Trinity elite and friends), and, one juicy night, reminded a couple of Kennedy cousins that they'd partied together one weekend earlier in the year. Brian had been big-time impressed. At Blend, the excellent new club in Provincetown, she'd spied her archrival, Taylor Ambrose, and her snippy sister Kiki—ha! As planned, she made sure to parade Brian in front of them.

Partly, she wanted word to get back to Lily that she was doing great without her (between air kisses and "Oh, my god, I love that dress!" convos, the subject of where she was living, or that she had a job, never came up). But mostly? Katie thrived on her life—did not want to think about the fact that she might not be enjoying this part of it for much longer.

Last night, Brian had taken her to The Naked Oyster in Hyannis. They'd washed down an entire seafood tower: clams, oysters, shrimp, lobster, and tuna sashimi—all Katie's favorites—with Stella Artois (for him), Perrier for her.

Twirling the straw in her drink, Katie'd toyed with confiding in him. Telling him the truth about her family, and asking for advice. And help. Maybe he'd have an idea, or simply excess cash he was willing to part with.

But Brian had wanted to go dancing. And at Fever, the nightclub of the moment, he'd run into a bunch of old frat buddies. Her moment was gone. By the time she got home at 3:15 a.m., she was too exhausted for a heart-to-heart; he was too inebriated to listen, anyway.

Joss smiled at her. "Glad you're having fun." As a joke, he asked, "We're all having fun, right?"

Mandy purred. A glance in her direction told Katie why. The tawdry tramp was flashing knowing eyes at *Joss*. Who blushed! They're sleeping together! Interesting. She would not have made that connection. As she headed back to room to change for "kitchen cleanup duty," she wondered again why Joss looked familiar.

### *Mandy Sees a New Friend.*

Mandy rose to toss her leftovers into the already overflowing garbage. And, to move farther away from piggy Ali and closer to Joss. His unshaven morning face, long, tousled hair, and drooping jeans turned her on. A guy like Joss, while not exactly her prey, could serve several useful purposes—already had.

Mandy was here to make contacts, not friends. And who knew? Bartender boy had recently been inside an actual showbiz orbit. Friend of an aging rock star was better than no important friends at all. And though she hadn't approached it directly yet, Mandy believed she could prevail upon Joss to hook her up with Jimi Jones. Better yet, his agent.

Why should Joss do her any favors? Well, she'd already—and quite successfully, if she did say so herself—given him a taste of what she brought to the table. So to speak.

For all her nineteen years, Mandy was no naïf. You had to give something to get something—that's how it worked. Especially in showbiz, it was all about who you knew. Or, in her case, who you could get to know quickly.

She'd worked a week's worth of swanky parties at Duck Creek Catering so far, and was, like, 0 for 6, netting no return on her slave-labor investment. Not that the mansions and resorts she'd gotten inside weren't something else! The clients were the disappointing part. Bunches of big ol' bores: corporate suits and their BOTOXed wives, or bankers, politicians, and stuffy New Englanders. Not a Kennedy or showbiz type in the bunch.

She'd had hopes for a Mr. Roger Durkin, at the Art Gallery party last week. He lived, he said, in California. His bank had insured the latest George Clooney movie. Mandy had popped another button on her top and started to tell him about her acting hopes, when Mrs. Insurance Guy rudely interrupted. So that was a bust. So to speak.

"He was so nice, so down to earth." Alefiya, talking to Joss, was describing the owner of a mansion her landscaping company was working for. "If my friend Jeremy hadn't told me, I never would have known he was such a big star. Meanwhile, he ordered a rock garden and waterfall, and a statue of a kid in the middle—guess what part of the anatomy the water's coming out of?"

Joss was laughing. "Man, that is lame. But there ya' go: Money doesn't buy taste. I'm surprised he's supervising it himself. Where's the million-dollar-a-year exterior designers?"

Mandy swung around. "You're working for a movie star?"

"He's from TV," Ali answered. "This guy who

used to be on *Friends*? He's from Boston originally. He lives in L.A. now, but when he was growing up, he dreamed of a place on the Cape. So now that he's a millionaire, he built this estate. I think his mom lives in it, but the other day he came out to talk to us himself."

Mandy was hyperventilating. She could feel Mitch's disapproving look behind her back, as well as Joss's bemused one. She didn't care. "Really? Have you met any of his . . . like, other celebrities?"

Ali cocked her head. "I'm the worst person to ask. I hardly pay attention to TV, so I might not recognize anyone. But Jeremy and some of the others on our crew worked at a bunch of celebrity homes last year and got friendly with a lot of people in that business."

Joss added, "Looks like Cove Landscaping is Cape Cod A-list. Turns out they made their reputation working for the Kennedys. Get this: Ali had to audition for the job by designing a mock topiary garden—shaped shrubs, the whole thing. Pretty cool, huh?"

Mitch couldn't restrain himself. "Hmmm, maybe you should have thought about growing vegetable canapés instead of passing them, Mandy."

Mandy didn't hear him. She hadn't gotten beyond "TV star" and "Kennedys." No matter how much blubber girl and her pet rat revolted her,

Mandy made a resolution: She was about to become Alefiya's new best friend.

### *Joss Grows Suspicious. With Good Reason.*

"Knock, knock. Anyone home?"

Mitch jumped, and was halfway out the kitchen before anyone could react. They heard him bolt through the living room and fling open the front screen door. "Leonora? Sweetheart! What a surprise!"

Joss knew this would be a good moment to make himself scarce. Mitch never let an opportunity pass when he could squeeze in an anecdote about Leonora. What were the odds he wasn't going to trot her in here, display her like some kind of trophy? Kind of like his own father paraded whatever number wife or girlfriend he was with, whenever he had an audience. Joss had no stomach for it. But he'd only managed a stride toward the archway leading to the living room when Mitch returned, beaming like a klieg light.

"Hey, everyone, this is Leonora, my girlfriend."

The chick on his arm was a photocopy of every debutante Joss had ever seen. Tall, thin, pale, bleached-white teeth, every golden hair in place. He noted the diamond tennis bracelet, the pearl necklace and matching stud earrings, and the Ralph

Lauren outfit. Uh-huh. This one was no poseur. Mitch had found himself the real old-money deal, but could he hope to keep up with her?

Leonora was seriously uncomfortable. Her body language—arms folded over her chest, pasted-on smile, pleading eyes—all shouted, "Get me out of here." She had not come to meet the housemates—that much, even Joss knew.

"Ah, the famous Leonora," Mandy said, dripping with phony interest and extending her hand, "we meet at last. Mitch talks about you all the time. And I'm not exaggerating when I say 'All. The. Time.'"

Leonora tossed her head slightly. "My sympathies. I can imagine how boring that must be."

"You said it, sister. Anyway, I'm Mandy, and this is my friend Ali." Joss shook his shaggy head. Mandy was a piece of work, all right. She'd done the fastest 180 he'd ever seen.

Ali advanced on Leonora and enveloped the startled girl in a bear hug, nearly crushing the bony thing. "I feel like we know you already! Mitch has the nicest things to say about you."

Leonora extracted herself quickly, smoothing out her blouse and stifling the look of alarm. She stuttered, "That's, uh . . . so sweet. Thanks."

"Would you like some coffee? Or bagels? There's a Cinnabon left too. Your boyfriend is the sweetest.

He brought breakfast for all of us." Ali motioned toward the spread on the kitchen counter.

"That's lovely," Leonora said, "but I really can't stay. I just stopped by to talk to Mitch and—"

"This is Joss." Mitch acted as if he hadn't heard his girlfriend at all. "Because of him, I'm not totally surrounded by gorgeous women. You should thank him."

Leonora managed a tight little smile. That's when Joss knew for sure something Mitch didn't. Something was askew in lovey-dovey land. He felt a pang and hoped that whatever was wrong with Miss Debutante wouldn't result in hurting Mitch. He was proudly shuttling "Lee" into the living room, insisting she meet Harper and Katie.

Joss eyed the two girls left in the kitchen with him. Mandy was street-smart and, he'd bet, had the same instincts as he did about Leonora. Ali? Nah. He sighed. It was time to do something he'd never done in his entire life.

Clean a bathroom.

# *Harper's Reverie*

Harper was psyched that she'd brought her bike, since Cape Cod was made for cyclists. Miles of paths, flat and hilly, laced the landscape, offering radically breathtaking scenery. She'd grown up on city streets, where the only nature was Central Park, if you didn't count the odd sprouts of weeds popping up between cracks in the sidewalk. Strange, but she found riding past the windswept sandy beaches and over grassy meadows a balm for her raw wounds.

She'd read somewhere that if you allow yourself to just empty your head, surrender to the grandeur of Mother Nature, your own problems seem smaller, your pain less intense.

Still waitin' to feel that way, she conceded.

Her aunt, twice widowed, believed in the opposite: that being frenetically busy, darting from one adventure to another, helped, "Because pain can't hit a moving target," she'd counseled.

Harper hunkered down and pedaled faster.

When she'd fled Boston for the summer, she hadn't been consciously thinking about anything beyond survival. 'Cause if she so much as glimpsed Luke, with or without his new squeeze, she would not be able to breathe. So she'd grabbed on to the first lifeboat she'd found: the Web posting that had led her here.

In a perverse way, Harper almost welcomed the bickering of the housemates, the carping of her campers; didn't even mind Katie as much as she made out. All the noise helped keep her mind off Luke. And where her mind went, maybe her heart would learn to follow.

Late Saturday afternoon, Harper was riding along one of her favorite daffodil-lined back roads into town. Her cell phone rang, and her stomach twisted. No way would it be Luke, she scolded herself. She had to stop hoping.

The caller ID read MOM.

Harper could swear her mother was a mind reader: Susan could see Harper and know what she was thinking, no matter how far apart they were.

"Where'd I catch you?" Susan asked. "On the beach somewhere?"

"Close. I'm biking into town to buy some stuff." Her list included orange juice, to make up for the half gallon that Ali had unintentionally taken from Katie. And the locksmith, so Mitch wouldn't find out that Ali had lost her keys—again.

Her mother wasn't big on small talk, anyway. Just a few minutes into the conversation, Susan launched into the real reason she'd called: Harper's heartbreak. "Keeping all that hurt bottled up inside won't help," said her mom, "and running away won't solve it."

Harper sighed. "So what will help, Mom? You're the expert."

Her mother didn't flinch. "Opening up, talking about how you feel. And time. Getting over him will take time."

How much time? Harper wanted to ask. How much time had it taken her mother to forgive her father, who'd said, "See ya" before Harper had been born?

When she'd first realized that all her friends had dads—even dads who didn't live with them—Harper had pleaded with her mom to get her one. For years, Susan had managed to change the subject artfully, to divert her attention, citing all the loving friends and relatives they did have.

Had her mother forgiven her father by that time?

Years later, when Harper was old enough to realize what any onlooker knew in an instant—that the sight of her with blond, blue-eyed Susan meant her father was likely African-American—she pushed harder to know the truth: "Who is he? Why can't I meet him?"

Reluctantly, Susan agreed to make contact. Days, weeks, then months went by—Harper had counted—with no reply, no news. Suspecting her mom hadn't made the call at all, Harper demanded to know her dad's identity.

When she was twelve, Susan told her his name.

Which only made Harper want to meet him more. He was famous! That made her important! And she, a street-smart New York kid, could do this without her mom's help. But Susan dissuaded her. "He was never a father to you," she'd said sadly. "I think of him as a sperm donor, that's all. I'm glad I got you out of it."

That's how she knew her mother, for all the time that had gone by, had never forgiven her father for walking out.

The following year, having bulked up on after-school specials and weepy TV movies, Harper had demanded, "Does he even know about me?"

Susan conceded that he did.

"Did he ever try to contact me?" Harper had probed, hoping maybe her father had wanted to but Susan had prevented him.

Susan had taken a deep breath. "Here's the thing, honey. At first, he tried to send money to help support you—which I'm sure his lawyer put him up to—but I refused it. I signed a waiver promising I'd never ask for anything, and never make it public. Because a scandal is exactly what he would've wanted—it would've given his bad-boy image some street cred. But I wasn't playing. I was no one's victim, and you were no one's pawn. You were mine."

Harper had learned all this just when her friends were beginning to date, just when boys at school had begun to notice her. It was a lucky crossroads. She, unlike so many of her teary, brokenhearted friends, knew from the jump not to trust boys, never to be vulnerable, never to open yourself up to that much hurt. She practiced what she believed.

Until Luke Clearwater came along.

"Guess what?" Harper said as she swung into the room she shared with Katie.

Her roommate was at the mirror—how new!—applying lip gloss. "Mmwhat?" Katie said while smushing her lips closed.

"You can float away on O.J. There's a ton in the fridge with your name."

Not taking her eyes off the mirror, Katie frowned. "You're not helping her by cleaning up her messes.

Even I stopped tossing away the half-eaten, fly-ridden fruit. I put them in her room instead."

"How thoughtful," Harper deadpanned. "I'm sure she appreciates that."

"That's not the point. Alefiya's never going to learn to be responsible for herself unless something impacts her directly."

This amused Harper. "Speaking of learning, how long do you think it'll take our Rebel Grllz to figure out your game?"

Katie bristled. "Since you've got it down, wanna clue me in?"

"That you could care less about them. That you're using them for their proximity to rich guys—and access to their parents' wallets." Harper hopped onto her bed.

"Your point?" Katie shrugged, continuing to separate and lengthen her lashes with her NARS mascara.

"It's not right, it's not moral. The only thing you're teaching them is how to shop and be manipulative."

"Who died and made you Oprah? The campers love me, and I'm not hurting anyone, so what's your issue?"

Seriously, Harper gave herself a mental jab: What *was* her issue? What did she care what Queen Katie did? It was true the campers worshipped Katie The Kick, from her silky platinum tresses to her cutesy designer sundresses. Katie was teaching them exactly what they wanted to learn, what most girls who came into contact with Katie wanted to know: how to be her.

As opposed to Harper's group, who were learning how to create the perfect protest poster, memorizing the ode to Barbie by Nerissa Nields ("If she were mortal, she would be/six foot five and a hundred and three,") and learning classic songs like "War, What Is It Good For?" and John Lennon's "Revolution."

Back to Katie, she mused. Why did the pocket-size princess need the money so badly? And why was she flinging herself at these random rich guys to get it? Didn't she have enough of both at home? This was the girl who, to Harper's amusement-slash-horror, *had brought her own toilet paper to the share house!* Like the community rolls weren't good enough to wipe her pampered butt. Katie tore from her own zillion-ply stash!

Harper sighed. Katie was crowding her head. She wandered out to the kitchen for a snack, where, unsurprisingly, more bickering was going on. Mitch was royally pissed at Ali, who apparently had left some chicken out to defrost—and had forgotten about it until the odor had stunk up the room. In related piss-off-iness, he was also questioning the number of guests she'd brought into the house. "What did you even know about that guy who was here last night? He looked homeless."

Ali shrugged. "He needed a place to crash."

"But this isn't a crash pad," Mitch reminded her. "It's our home for the summer."

"Exactly," Joss had tossed in, though no one had asked him, "*our* home. Ali's one of us. She has rights too."

Mitch looked betrayed. He was about to say something, but never got the chance. An eardrum-piercing, roof-raising series of shrieks shook the house. Mandy. She'd been on the toilet, apparently, when Clarence the ferret pushed the door open with his nose and leaped into her bare lap. Now she was running to her room, screeching at the top of her lungs. Her capris were down around her ankles and, Harper envisioned, pee was running down her thigh.

It was time for a "moment of Zen."

Armed with her journal and a big bath towel, Harper headed out. The narrow ribbon of sand backing onto the share house could barely be called a beach. It was grassy, and full of weeds. Harper came here often, especially at times like now, at dusk, when she had it all to herself.

She could hear the splashes of birds ducking and

fishing in the surf, the rhythm of the waves lapping onto the shore. If the night happened to be clear, she could write by moonlight. That wouldn't be the case tonight. The sky had been tinny all day, the air thick with humidity. It'd rain soon. The gloom matched her mood.

Her relationship with Luke Clearwater had started as a friendship. Two outsiders bonding over poetry, writing. They'd met at Barnes & Noble. She'd been sitting on the floor, blocking the narrow aisle with Maya Angelou's inspirational *And Still I Rise* spread on her knees. People stepped around her, or over her, mumbling annoyed *"excuse me"*'s. Luke had knelt down next to her, clutching a copy of *The Collected Poems of Langston Hughes*. And for the next hour, shoppers had to avoid stepping on both of them.

It was through the words, then, written by others, that Harper and Luke had scripted their own love story. It had all seemed so organic.

And simple. He *got* her. Understood her passions because he shared so many of them. He wasn't put off by her moods—as her mom constantly reminded her, she was either sulky or sarcastic, serious or angry. She trusted Luke with her ideas, her own poetry, her real self. He responded kindly and constructively, admitting that "My Brother" (a poem reflecting Harper's longing for a sibling) made him cry. He'd helped her with one called "Flat," wondering if the poem about spiritual death wouldn't be more powerful if she killed that middle verse.

Harper had taken a big breath, and a bigger chance, exposing her soul to him. It was her first time.

Harper helped Luke, too. He was a senior at Boston Latin High School and delivered pizza after school, but he had the soul of a writer. Unfortunately, he had trouble stitching his profound, but scattered thoughts into a cohesive story. She'd worked on that with him, forcing him to think through what he wanted to say. "If you can think it, you can write it," Harper counseled.

Dude, she'd done good by him. One short story got published in *The New Yorker* magazine; an essay got selected for NPR, National Public Radio. Not that any of the kids at school would've heard of it. But both the literary magazine and the radio station were big, big deals. With Harper's encouragement, Luke had just sent a collection to a literary agency, hoping maybe some agent would sign him up.

Their relationship had its physical side. Harper loved the way Luke kissed her—soul kisses that could last for days, as he'd written. And she loved the way he touched her, slowly, lovingly, all over.

He was willing to wait, he'd said, for the rest. He was willing to wait, he'd said, for her to be ready.

Until the day he'd casually said, "See ya," and walked out of her life.

Stunned, paralyzed, Harper had begged to know why. It wasn't about sex, he'd assured her.

It was worse.

He'd found another muse. His *real* soul mate.

A raindrop, or maybe a tear, squiggled down her check, dripped onto her open journal, and pooled on the page, blurring an entire paragraph. Harper used the corner of her towel to blot it up, and dabbed her eye as well. Even alone, she did not want to cry over him. It was *not*, contrary to popular pop-psychology belief, cathartic. In spite of what she wanted, the tears kept coming. She closed her journal, and let them—and the rain, for it was drizzling now—have their way.

Sometime later, over her sniffles, she heard the squeak of the backyard fence open and close, followed by squishy footsteps through the wet grass. Harper froze.

"I looked all over, but I couldn't find an umbrella in the house. Brought the next best thing."

Harper turned her head and squinted. Through her blobby-wet eyelashes she saw Joss, a Yankees cap shielding his head from the rain. He was offering her one with a SPRINGSTEEN logo. He was toting a bottle of wine and a paper bag.

He looked so ridiculous, this reedy-thin hippie

longhair in his torn jeans, faded Rolling Stones T-shirt, and baseball cap coming to "rescue" her. She started to laugh through her tears.

"Was it something I said?" Joss knelt next to her in the wetly packed sand as she took the alt rain hat from him.

"Just a surreal moment." She was grateful, and stuffed as much as she could of her springy hair under the cap. "So what, you looked outside and saw me sitting in the rain?" Harper hoped that hadn't come out as an accusation.

"Pretty much, yeah. And from experience? Girls rarely enjoy getting their hair wet unless there's a swimming pool nearby."

"True dat," Harper conceded. She nodded at the wine bottle. "On your way out?"

"I managed to liberate some libations, a lively little Bordeaux, along with some hors d'ouevres, courtesy of The Naked Oyster. Thought you might want."

Suddenly, Harper was salivating. "Did you bring a corkscrew?"

He reached into his back pocket and pulled out a Swiss Army knife.

"A Boy Scout," Harper said, making room for him on her blanket. "Who'd a thunk?"

"Never made it past Cub Scouts. I'm not big on anything organized."

Harper peered into the paper bag. "All right!

Real imitation cheese-food. And one hundred percent artificial Doritos. Perfect."

"Hey, the price was right." Joss freed the cork from the bottle.

Harper grinned and took the wine from his outstretched hand. She wasn't much of a drinker; a random beer pretty much summed up the extent of her experience. Time to widen her horizons. She closed her eyes, hoisted the bottle to her lips, took a swig, and nearly spit it out. "Vinegar, much?"

Joss laughed. "You should see your face." He handed her a cube of cheese. "Can't be that bad. We charge something like eight dollars a glass for this."

"Dude, your customers are getting robbed," she said, wiping her mouth and watery eyes on her sweatshirt sleeve. "But as long as it does its job, I'm all over it."

"Self-medicating?" Josh guessed.

"I'll let you know if it works." She handed it back to him.

"It will—temporarily, at least," he assured her.

"Temporary will do. For now."

"So, anyway," Joss said, "I'm thinking you came out here to be alone. I'll split. Unless you feel like talking. There's a strict code of bartender-client privilege. What goes in here"—he pointed to his ear—"stays in here. If not, they revoke my license."

Harper giggled. He was trying to be cute. But on

the real, Joss must be privy to a whole mess of sagas. A summer's worth of lonely hearts confessionals. Boozy babes coming on to him, loser dudes confiding their frustration at "never getting any." Harper could hear it all now. She would trust him? Not so much. But she *was* curious. "You like bartending?"

"It's cool. Between the gig and the share house, I get to stay put for a few months."

Harper was about to ask what he did when he wasn't staying in one place, when the loud crash of smashing glass made them jump. It came from behind them—the house. And now Mitch yelling, Ali pleading, and Mandy bursting her vocal cords.

Joss leaped up. "Better see what happened. Be right back."

Harper thought about going with him, but what could she do? Alefiya's laissez-faire attitude was going to rile Mitch all summer.

Joss returned about ten minutes later. "It seems, in a gross violation of house rules, the ferret got free—and, as usual, Mandy lost it. One freaked-out ferret, and one large table lamp. You do the math."

"Equals," she quipped, "one apoplectic Mitch, one pissed-off bitch, and one Hindu pitching excuses about how the Not-a-Rodent just got scared?"

"That's rich." Joss kept the rhyming beat. "Poetry and irony—comes naturally to you, does it?"

Harper squirmed. "And what part did Katie play

in today's episode of our daily domestic drama?"

"Bailed. I saw her duck out the door just as I got there."

"Typical." Harper tsk-tsked. "The queen of control doesn't like when things get messy. Her game is strictly passive-aggressive."

"I thought you were her friend."

"Not even remotely," Harper confessed. "She goes to my high school, she posted a Web ad, and I answered. End of story."

"So you and Katie are two agendas passing in the night, huh? I'm guessing you didn't like her much back in high school," Joss speculated.

"I don't like her much now. She's a self-centered, materialistic, lying, manipulative opportunist. A conniving witch in Abercrombie clothing who brings her own designer toiler paper to a crappy share house."

"But tell us what you really think, Harper," Joss cracked, taking another swill of the wine.

"Oh, come on, tell me you like her," Harper challenged. "Word to the wise, if you do—you're not her type. She's all about the money, honey. Working slobs need not apply."

Joss paused, as if crafting his answer required careful thought. Finally, he said, "I don't really know Katie. But I know her type. She probably feels she has to pretend everything's groovy even when things totally suck. It's a hard ruse to keep up."

Harper mimed playing the violin.

Joss laughed. "Point taken."

"Katie can fend for herself; girlfriend has got it all under control. It's Alefiya I'm worried about. Granted, she's messy, spacy—and forgetful. But she's good people, compassionate, generous, just real." Harper looked to Joss for validation. She found it in his furrowed brow. "The others can't stand her—I'm worried they might drive her out, do something really hurtful."

"Housemates," Josh deadpanned. "Can't live with 'em. Can't set 'em on fire."

Harper broke into peels of laughter, slapped the sand. "Good one."

Joss started to bury the now drained wine bottle. "My money's on Mitch, for the one with the troubled road ahead."

"Why? He's probably the most together of us."

"That's what he thinks too—and that's the problem."

Harper looked at him quizzically. "Do you know something?"

"Just what I feel," Joss admitted. "T'ain't pretty."

Maybe it was the buzz of the wine, or that Joss actually worried about other people—including herself—sitting out in the rain. But for the first time, she took real note of him. "Where are you from?"

"Nowhere in particular."

"Everyone's from somewhere," she scoffed, hoping he'd say New York.

"Mostly, I travel."

"A real wanderer," Harper mused, "from place to place, bar to bar, supporting yourself as it comes?"

"Something like that." Joss pointed to her journal. "And you? Poet? Writer?"

"Something like that."

The rain, never more than a steady drizzle, had settled for full-out mist, from which moonbeams now poked. And Harper found herself opening up—just a crack—to Joss. She admitted to writing, and yes, poetry was her thing. Why? No concrete reason. There was something about the way he looked at her, and who it *didn't* remind her of. Luke had been full of passion. He'd been smitten by Harper, and wore it on his sleeve. Not Joss. Joss seemed genuinely curious. Interested.

She found she was too.

# 10

## *Monday, Joss Plays a Hunch*

The night Joss joined Harper on the beach was not the first time he'd spied her out there alone.

It was the first time he had an excuse to go to her, be alone with her, get to know her. He wasn't into her in a sexual way, he didn't think. It was more an itch he couldn't scratch: Something about her continued to intrigue him. It seemed important to figure it out.

For her part, the sarcastic and contrary room-mate—the one he'd nicknamed Angry Young Babe—was grateful for his company. He still couldn't nail who she reminded him of, but sitting close to her, talking, joking, swilling some wine, he'd learned a lot.

Someone had broken her heart; she didn't need

to come out and tell him. But she was grieving. Still, she'd been funny, and smart and creative. Instinct told him that she was musical. Poetry, yeah. Put it to music, you call it lyrics. He'd bet anything she played *something*. Piano, possibly; guitar, more likely.

Lying in bed that night, Joss suddenly had a hunch about Harper. He decided to follow up on it in his spare time.

Not that he had a lot. Mostly, he was working, or otherwise engaged. Late nights he was at the bar, and even later nights he found plenty of distractions. Or rather, they found him.

Women had always told him he was sexy. How many of his father's bimbettes had secretly come on to him? Joss had stopped counting long ago. With girls his own age, it was the same deal. All through prep school, he'd been the catch, the meat, the prime, grade-A hunk. The big "get."

It did nothing for him. It was like this macho joke his dad used to repeat: A sexy young starlet approaches a big-time Hollywood agent at a party. She says, "Come upstairs and I'll give you the best b.j. you've ever had." The agent replies, "Yeah, but what's in it for me?"

Joss could not conceive of being that cruel to anyone, but like so many charismatic guys, he got the joke. He'd walked out on that life. No one knew him here, and yet women were drawn to him just the same. They found him mysterious, intriguing. That was cool. There were no strings, expectations, or pretenses. Just fun flings, safe and anonymous.

The one he regretted was Mandy. "Never shit where you eat." Another of Father's Favorite Filthy Clichés. Meaning, getting involved with someone at work, or who lived nearby, was doomed to end in disaster.

Between him and Mandy it was like this: Nights she came home disappointed, frustrated, pissed off—pretty much her three main moods—she came knocking at his door. A booty call.

It had only been a few times, but Joss was ready to knock it off. The momentary pleasure—he'd always been a sucker for redheads—wasn't worth the potential complications. For one thing, it prevented him from bringing another girl to the house, should he want to. It'd be too weird. For another, secrets weren't likely to remain so for long. The walls were paper thin, Mandy's mouth anything but.

Mandy Starr—yeah, talk about made-up names—was crass, but she was also cagey. He'd already told her too much, especially the part about being a roadie with Jimi Jones. He wished he hadn't disclosed that. She was digging for backstory like a dog pawing for a bone, and if she came up with even a partial truth, his cover was shot. Very uncool.

Something else was happening to Joss, something heady and amazing. He'd found a spot, a cove on a beach in Wellfleet. Afternoons, or those predawn hours after work, he'd started going there, just him and the old acoustic, the cheapest of his collection. On that sandy beach, he didn't have to push, to struggle. Music came to him. And stayed! Tunes composed themselves in his head there, while he was pretending to listen to someone's sob story at the bar, while he was making small talk with some babe, even while he was asleep. He put them all down in his PDA and at his first opportunity tried them out on guitar. Damn! This was this first real creative streak. What a rush!

### Tuesday Night, Katie Goes Out—<br>Er . . . Stays In—With Brian.

"Hell yeah, I'm taking the summer off," Brian Holloway was telling Katie. "I deserve it." Late afternoon, with camp officially over for the day, Katie joined Brian by the pool, a habit she'd fallen into, and he welcomed. She usually found him stretched out on a chaise lounge—the very same one he'd occupied when Katie'd first laid eyes on him and looking every bit as luscious—coolly sipping a margarita.

She hadn't had to prod much to get Brian to open up about himself. Upon graduation, he would go into the family business, starting as a junior executive in his dad's fund-management business. "So this is my break, The Summer of Brian," he said now, without irony. "Probably the last summer of my life I'll be able to do exactly what I want, with no obligations."

From her own padded lounge chair, Katie leaned over to run her fingers through his thick inky curls. "I don't believe you," she said in her flirtiest tone. "I bet your whole life you've done exactly as you wanted."

Brian grinned. "Busted. So I'm being lazy for a few months. I still think I deserve it."

Katie, though sweaty and tired from her long day—getting her group ready for a Camp Olympics, she'd been on the run all day from swim practice to tennis to track—playfully licked his earlobe. "Wanna know what I deserve?"

Brian looked at her hopefully.

"Dinner."

He laughed. "Are you kidding?" He checked his Tourneau watch, which Katie had calculated was worth at least $4,000. "It's not even six. Give me a break, I only got up a few hours ago. But I'll order you a drink—"

Katie shook her head. The idea of a frothy fruity alcoholic mix was so not what she craved right now. A steak was more like it.

Brian said soothingly, "You look tired. Come

snuggle with me, I'll make room here, and you can sip my drink. I'll get the waiter to bring us some chips."

"I don't think so," Katie demurred. "I'm kinda sweaty."

Brian winked. "Oooh, I like that in a girl."

Katie rolled her eyes, knowing she looked adorable. "Really, Brian. I was out in the sun all day with the campers and didn't get a chance to shower. And I am ravenous."

He bolted straight up. "Ravenous, huh? Well, when you put it that way . . ."

"Not kidding. Really starving."

"Okay, how 'bout this, then? Come up to my suite and take a shower. Then, we'll go out to eat. Dinner for you, breakfast for me. How's that?"

Brian was so amazing, between that jet-black hair, startling blue eyes, soft lush pillow lips, it was hard for Katie to keep her eyes off him. He knew how to treat a girl too. He had an agenda? What guy didn't? Katie could deal.

She had her own agenda (sort of). Without Lily, the plan wasn't exactly formulated. She kept hoping an idea would come to her. In the meantime, parading around the Cape with Brian Holloway was most excellent. By now, he knew she worked as a counselor at the Luxor, but he totally bought she was doing it to fulfill this "social consciousness" thing for her mother's "organization."

Later, after she'd indeed showered, riffled through Brian's drawers, and wrapped herself in one of his shirts and boxer shorts, he did treat her to a huge steak and crispy French fries. Via room service.

"We can't go out," he'd argued, putting some Norah Jones on the in-room stereo, "unless you want to wear my clothes. Which you look delectable in, by the way."

Well, duh. Coyly, Katie put her hands on her tiny waist and replied, "I thought I'd be showering and changing at my place, then we'd go out."

Brian, of course, had other thoughts, other intentions—only some of which Katie was willing to give in to. Not that he wasn't an incredible kisser. Brian kissed with his eyes closed, his long lashes tickling her cheek. Wrapping her in his arms, he always started slowly, with tiny pecks, then gently opened her lips—at which point their tongues took over. They seemed to know how to slow dance all by themselves. It felt good, it felt right, it felt like she could do *that* all night.

It also felt too soon. It was still early in the summer, and Katie couldn't risk things moving too quickly. Besides, Nate might still be in the game—not that Brian knew it—and there were times, she had to admit, when her thoughts wandered to swapping saliva with him. Would he taste salty?

Tonight, she was having a mental threesome.

Joss bothered her. She was still annoyed about last Saturday night. So what if she'd left the house in the middle of another of Ali's messes and Mandy's melodramas? Not her issue. Yet Joss had shot her this accusing look, like she was leaving the scene of a crime. Who was he to judge her (if that's what he was doing), anyway? He was hardly without secrets of his own. Maybe the others were clueless—Harper certainly was—but Katie knew what was going on between Joss and Mandy. If only she could remember how she knew him from before the share house.

### Wednesday, The Beach Is Back.

Mandy was jazzed. After three frustrating weeks, *finally* something was about to go her way. That her good fortune was coming courtesy of the slobo next door was an unexpected twist. But she was used to adjusting.

Mandy could barely stand to look at her—let alone her repulsive rodent—but Alefiya Sunjabi was about to become Mandy's bestest friend. At least until Porky Pig delivered a well-connected client capable of jump-starting her career.

Wednesday, Ali's day off, Mandy called in sick to Duck Creek Catering and invited her NBF to hang out with her. "I'm going to Craigville Beach, the meatpacking district. If you know what I mean."

Alefiya did not.

Mandy winked conspiratorially. "An all-you-can-eat buffet of grade-A prime, guys with packages you would not believe. A girl could get lucky."

Well, *she* could get lucky—if she wanted. In her uplifting white-and-gold-studded bikini, Mandy was a guy magnet. Whereas Ali, she guessed, would be lucky not to be mistaken for a beached whale. It was win-win.

"Sounds like good times," Ali had said agreeably.

Mandy's description of Craigville Beach may have been crude, but it was accurate. She'd heard locals call it "Muscle Beach," one of the few on the Cape not designated "family friendly." For the buff and the beautiful, the predators and their willing prey, it was packed with hard bodies wearing smooth tans and skimpy swimwear. It was scope-out, hook-up city. Where better, Mandy thought, for the new "girlfriends" to get all confidential?

Along with her lip gloss, Mandy packed several bottles of water, a Ziploc bag of celery stalks, the latest issue of *Us* magazine, sunscreen, and an umbrella for herself—she burned easily.

Ali lugged a big picnic basket, filled with messy mayonnaise-y salads, tuna sandwiches, and iced tea. Obviously, she hadn't gotten the memo that Mandy didn't do carbs. Ali had also toted some gi-normous, scratchy-looking blanket, as if they were going to share. Yeah, right.

Mandy snagged a strategic spot for them, midway between two groups of guys, tricked out with beer cooler, MP3 players, wandering eyes, and appreciative smiles. As she shimmied out of her cover-up, she watched Ali peel off her elastic-band shorts and T-shirt, hoping the plump girl hadn't committed a fashion fiasco by wearing a two-piece. Even one of those old-lady types with a skirt would be better.

Surprisingly, Ali wore a black V-neck maillot, as flattering to her figure as a girl her size could get. "Not what you expected, huh?" Ali said, reading Mandy's mind. "Better, or worse?"

"I . . . uh . . . ," she stuttered. "You look . . . good."

"For someone my size, right? That's what you were thinking?"

"No way!" Mandy lied.

"Forget it. I don't have body issues the way a lot of girls do. I'm lucky."

Looking to change the subject swiftly, Mandy nodded toward a toned and taut twosome on the next blanket over, one in a slinky Speedo, the other in tantalizing trunks. "Speaking of bodies, check it out."

Ali licked her lips. "I wouldn't kick either one out of bed."

Mandy was, what, scandalized? Even knowing Ali brought home every stray on the Cape, Mandy didn't believe she actually slept with any of them. A girl of her heritage and heft was more likely to be a guy's friend, not his squeeze.

Ali laughed, going all mind reader on her again. She laughed. "I'm Hindu, and big—so people assume I'm sheltered, a virgin. But"—she put her finger to her cheek—"I'm guessing people make wrong assumptions about you, too?"

No way was Mandy going there—especially not with Buddha. There were limits to this newfound friendship.

"It's okay." Ali shrugged, rubbing sunscreen onto her ample arms. "We're all guilty of stereotyping, even me."

A perfect segue to gossiping about their house-mates, and Mandy was just about to, only "Beep, beep!" Her "guy-dar" went off. The incoming hottie was mouthwateringly broad-shouldered, slim-waisted, and tousled-haired. She shifted position to pose languidly for optimum cleavage effect.

He was still several feet away when he waved. "Yo, Alefiya! Howzit hangin'?"

Mandy nearly fell out of her top. He . . . knew . . . *her?*

"Jeremy!" Ali jumped up and ran to hug him.

Jeremy. Mandy did a mental Google. Wasn't he

the one who'd worked at Cove Landscaping for several years, knew all the celebs? She leaped to her feet.

Ali made the intros. Mandy purred, "A pleasure to meet you, Jeremy Davis. Ali has told us so much about you. Come join us. We'll make it worth your while."

A slow, if surprised, smile played across Jeremy's lips. "You guys are friends?"

Mandy laughed. "As of today, we are!" Then she added, "Seriously, we've got eats and drinks, way too much for the two of us."

Jeremy unscrewed a bottle of iced tea and settled on Ali's blanket, which now seemed inviting to Mandy, and she squeezed in. She politely allowed them a few minutes of flower-speak, or whatever lawn-yawn stuff they were yapping about. Finally, she interrupted. "It must be so exciting in your job, getting to meet celebrities and important people."

Jeremy gave Ali a sideways glance and shrugged. "Uh, sure. I mean, they're really just like everyone else. Once you get to know them."

Animated now, Mandy leaned closer to Jeremy. "That's what I always say! I know I'd hit it off with them. I mean, take me, for example. . . ." She paused, lightly resting her hand on his muscled forearm. "You could probably tell I'm a model. But I have so much more to offer. Only, breaking into acting is so hard! It's all about connections, who you know. That's how everyone gets started."

After that, it hadn't taken much time for Jeremy to agree to introduce Mandy to some guys he hung out with, friends of friends, sons of the quasifamous and connected.

That was all she'd wanted. Her "bonding" with Ali? Over it. She sure didn't need what came next. Ali, clapping her hands and bouncing up and down like a blubbery seal. "We should have a party! For the Fourth of July—you bring your friends, I'll invite some other people from Cove, and we'll mix it up. Saturday night at our place—you can introduce Mandy to everyone at the same time."

"But the Fourth was over a week ago," Mandy noted.

Ali shrugged. "It's always the right time to celebrate independence, no? Fourth, fourteenth, twenty-fourth—what's the difference?"

"Works for me." Jeremy was enthusiastic. "Give me the address, we'll bring some fireworks."

"Three-four-five Cranberry Lane," Ali told him. "Come around ten."

With a peck on the cheek for Ali and a nod to Mandy, Jeremy got up to rejoin his friends.

When he was out of earshot, Mandy said, "You really think a party's such a good idea? It isn't really necessary, I could just—"

Ali waved her away. "As long as we don't tell Mitch. The poor guy is so uptight. What he doesn't know won't stress him." She started rambling about baking Brie, making tostados, and stocking the fridge with beer, when Mandy tuned out. What would she wear?

Mandy got up and stretched. "I'm going for a swim."

"In the ocean? For real?" Ali looked doubtful.

"No, not for real. In the movie," she deadpanned, turned, and ran toward the surf. The foamy water swirled around her ankles and, like always, made her feel safe. She rushed in and began strong, swift strokes that carried her out into the ocean. Mandy flashed back on the pool at the Dorchester Boys and Girls Club, where she'd learned to swim. The one silver lining in her otherwise crappy childhood: The exercise had peeled layers of fat off her.

### Thursday, Mitch Showers With Worry.

Creeping worry. The knowing that something's wrong—or about to be . . . only you don't know what it is. It had plagued Mitch all his life. He'd learned to cope by swatting it away, peeling it off, beating it into submission until he could figure out what it was and deal with it. Right now, as he took his post-jog shower, he tried to scrub it away like dirt before it got under his skin and infected him.

This worry-bug had a name: Leonora. The morning his girl had shown up at the house had been such a sweet surprise. En route to a tennis game, she'd stopped off to see him first. She never did say why she needed to see him. Later, on the phone, she got angry and accused him of never giving her the chance to talk. "I came by because I needed to see you alone," she'd said, growling when he'd chuckled suggestively.

"Not for that reason!" she growled. "I didn't have a lot of time, and you totally wasted it by showing me off to those people you live with, like some prize."

Wincing at her condescending tone toward "those people you live with," Mitch nevertheless conceded. "You *are* my prize. Of course I want to show you off. I love you. What's wrong with that?"

"Your timing, that's what!" She hung up on him.

Lee was normally sweet-tempered, so he figured the outburst might be PMS-related. Growing up with a twin sister, he knew about female moodiness. Leonora's had not been pretty. She stayed annoyed with him, punishing him by canceling their date that night. That same night, the stupid ferret had broken the lamp, which led to his own outburst. He'd charged Ali for the damage, but felt guilty all the same.

Ah well, another weekend was a couple of days away, and Lee had softened, promising to spend it with him. She did need to talk to him, she'd said.

"About what?" he'd asked.

"About us."

Creeping worry. Mitch scrubbed harder. Whatever she was mad at, he'd make it right. He was her boyfriend, soon-to-be fiancé. Making things right with her was his job. And his joy.

### Friday, Harper Runs Into Leonora.

TGIF! The Rebel Grllz had decided to have a weekly "Thank Goddess It's Friday" event. The idea had been Katie's—big surprise—but they had done the democratic thing and voted on the plans. Katie's crew always united in opting to shop every week. Harper had tried, and failed, to urge her bunch to widen their horizons, see a play, attend a concert, a trip to Provincetown: some culture.

"Shopportunities." Katie coined a word, and won. Again.

Today marked the third Friday they crammed into the resort's minibus and headed out to satisfy the primal needs of the eager little consumers. Harper was still holding out hope that eventually she'd have some positive influence on the group, but times like these, they were all about the tops, the shoes, the 'cessories.

Harper *had* won the smallest of battles. At least they weren't going to another brain-numbing Galleria, but into the town of Dennisport, checking out funkier shops, vintage clothing, local arts and crafts.

On the bus, Harper sat next to her favorite camper, Gracie Hannigan. Shy Gracie wasn't as superficial as the others, but that wasn't the real reason Harper took to her. The child had issues: self-esteem, body, braces, geeky glasses—the usual tween traumas—only she wasn't very good at hiding them. Which made her prime prey for the others, who delighted in making themselves feel good by making her feel bad. Gleefully, the baby-fashionistas pointed out that stripes, tights, baby tees, or flip-flops were so over! And didn't Gracie know—hello!—that capris were played? And who cut her hair, the lawn guy?

The taunts weren't new to the kid; she'd suffered verbal poison darts in school, too. But that didn't make them hurt less. If only, Harper caught herself thinking, Gracie was thin. She wasn't.

Gracie reacted by trying to blend in. As Harper had read in a book somewhere, she'd turned self-effacing to self-erasing. She never spoke up for herself.

Harper's strategy was to bring out Gracie's talents, her artistry, her musical chops. Good idea, in concept. In the real world of eleven-year-olds? The only way Gracie could hope to survive was to fight with the same ammo: Harper secretly hoped they'd find something on this excursion—some necklace, or top, or hair accessory—that'd boost the kid's self-esteem.

Luck was with them. Just a few hours into the shop-op, Harper scored better than she'd dared hope. She'd found Gracie this boho retro outfit—cute top and pants—and it fit! All the girls complimented her, told her how rad she looked. Harper spent her own money to add a necklace, and bracelet to match.

The little girl was truly aglow for the first time all summer. And so was Harper.

On the bus ride home, two of the other campers decided to style Gracie's hair so it'd go with her new look. So psyched, Gracie could barely wait to get back to the Luxor. "I can't wait to show my mom. Harper, you have to come with me!"

Harper didn't want to—she was tired, and what if Gracie's mom didn't approve or something? But she couldn't say no to Gracie's pleas. "You have to be there when my mom sees me. Pleeeze, puleeze, pretty please."

What ensued was neither, Harper would think later, pretty nor pleasing. When they got back, she followed the kid into the hotel and waited outside the ladies' room in the lobby while her camper put on her new outfit and accessories. Counselor and camper took the elevator up to the ninth floor, down the corridor to Suites 909–910, the executive area where Gracie's family resided for this summer. Because she wanted the surprise to be total, Gracie didn't knock, but used her key.

There was a surprise all right—on them.

Gracie's mom wasn't in. Her dad was. In bed, undressed, and uh . . . cuddling. With someone who wasn't Gracie's mom.

But who was Leonora.

# Alefiya Gets This Party Started— The Fireworks Go Off!

*"I'm comin' up, so you better get this party started. . . ."*

The sky over the ocean outside 345 Cranberry Lane was clear and quiet. Its annual gig as host to the big fireworks display was over weeks ago.

This night, the fireworks were indoors.

It was close to midnight, and Ali's Not-the-Fourth-of-July party was off the hook, slammin'! There were easily, she calculated, a hundred people—and their dancin' feet—crammed in. Music rocked the rafters; food and drink flowed generously. Everyone was dancing, drinking, eating, and socializing. Interesting combinations of legs, arms, and other body parts intertwined as people squished together on the couches, chairs, tabletops, fireplace mantel, any inch of space they could find. The kitchen, where the bar had been set up and where she'd stashed most of "Alefiya's Incredible Edibles," was just as crowded. Hook-ups were happening in the bedrooms—she'd seen couples sneaking off—even the bathrooms were "occupied."

Ali, wearing a traditional sari with a red, white, and blue do-rag on her head, was sandwiched on the sofa between Jeremy and Sharif. She had never been this ecstatic—or, for that matter, stoned—in her entire nineteen years. This, she thought, deeply inhaling the joint the trio were sharing, is exactly how she'd imagined her summer, back when she'd planned it. "Schemed" was maybe the better word.

For the first time, she'd been able to get away from her parents, grandparents, uncles, aunts, cousins, siblings—her great big, colorful, opinionated family. She loved them all to death, and basically, totally respected their values, her heritage. But there were certain issues. Like the fact that her family insisted she become a doctor, and forbade her from fraternizing with any boy who wasn't Indian.

What could a wholesome, assimilated girl do? She was all about helping people, but preferred buds and stems to blood and stem cells. As for guys, she fell in and out of love every day; she was color-blind.

When the time came, maybe she would marry a "respectable" Indian boy, as her parents wished. But the time wasn't now. These three delicious months she'd fashioned into her own personal *rumspringa*, an Amish concept she'd brazenly co-opted. This was her first true Independence Day, her taste of real freedom. It tasted better than anything she'd ever tried. Even hot-from-the-oven Cinnabons.

"*. . . Pumpin' up the volume with this brand new beat . . .*"

Jeremy's arm was flung around her shoulders, and Sharif was leaning into her side. Ali felt incredibly connected to every single person in the house, especially her roommates.

The one twinge of guilt: Mitch. She'd pulled this fiesta off behind his back, and against his big-ass rules. She wished she hadn't had to go covert, but he wasn't likely to show up tonight. He was finally spending the weekend at Leonora's.

Neither Katie nor Joss had arrived yet, but Ali was sure they'd dive right in. How much fun was this? She noticed Mandy, swathed in some hot pink confection with a daringly deep V-neck, animatedly chatting up someone she assumed was Jeremy's friend. Ummm . . . chatting up? More like brushing up against, curling herself around. Soul-patch dude seemed familiar, but Ali was in no shape to nudge a brain cell awake and attempt recall.

Ali saw Harper leaning against the far wall, surveying the room. Her fists were shoved inside the upper pockets of her cargo pants. She was wearing a T-shirt with the slogan, PAIN WAS TOO GOOD FOR HIM. It matched her sour expression. Uh-oh, Ali ought to go see what was wrong, but du-u-u-ude, as Jeremy would say, she was just soooo comfortable exactly where she was.

*"It's gettin' hot in here . . . so take off all your clothes."*

Jeremy licked her ear, which made her giggle. And Sharif—or "Reef," as he liked to be called these days—had just made room on his lap for his girlfriend, Lisa. Ali leaned over Jeremy to pass the joint, when something disturbed her full and total inner peace moment.

"Al*ee*-fee-ya." Someone was calling her, someone whose bouncy tone belied a disapproving 'tude.

"Excuse me, but what exactly is going on?" There it was again. Through her sweet and savory haze of marijuana, she realized (a) that line was not part of Nelly's party anthem, and (b) she should know the person asking the question.

Only she wasn't sure. She sighed, threw her head back on the couch, and closed her eyes, letting a satisfied smile spread across her face.

"Earth to Alefiya. I repeat, what's going on here?" The voice again, rising, trembling now. Ali tried to figure out who it was as she took hold of the joint Jeremy passed to her.

*"Mix a little bit a ah, ah . . . with a little bit a ah, ah."*

"Ouch!" Someone had kicked her in the shin? She coughed out the choking smoke, nearly gagging, her eyes tearing.

"Alefiya! What's going on?"

More puzzled than perturbed, Ali looked up and tried to focus. She registered long, straight strands of gossamer hair brushing bare shoulders. Then, round baby-blue eyes, clouded over in rage, reddened cheeks, and rosebud lips pressed together tightly.

Katie! *That's* who it was. Katie standing above her, hands on her tiny hips, feigning curiosity about the party. A little vein in Katie's forehead was throbbing—Ali had never noticed that before. Did it mean Katie was actually angry, even though she didn't want to sound mad? Why? Had she forgotten to invite her? But that was impossible! Katie lived here. She was invited by default. So why was—

"I need to speak to you, now." Katie forced a smile.

Ali mustered, "Cool! Jeremy's lap's available. Sit yourself down!"

"Alone," Katie clarified.

"Yo, Leaf," Jeremy whispered, using the nickname he'd made up, "she looks serious."

His whispering tickled her ear, and she burst out laughing. Sharif stilled her. "Come on, I'll help you up." He nudged Lisa off his own lap.

Why was Katie squeezing her elbow so hard?

Who knew the elfin girl was that strong, anyway? She was practically pushing her through the packed room, not even letting her pause to hug her friends from work, Jason and Eddie, and that nice guy she'd met at the bar the other night whose name escaped her.

Ali wanted to ask Mandy if the guy she was draped around was the famous photographer. And oh, Harper! She totally needed to talk to her. But Katie wasn't slowing down, just kept forcing her forward, through the throng, shouting, "Excuse us, move, please, excuse us." They were headed toward the kitchen. Ali was trying to tell Katie that that was not the place to find privacy. Dude! That's where the kegs were! And the lime shots and the vodka, tequila, rum, and fruity drinks. Didn't Katie realize it'd be even more crowded there?

Katie eased her vise grip when they did hit the kitchen—and then, only because the floor was slippery. And Katie sort of . . . went flying. Landing on her . . . what was that word Ali found so hilarious? Keister! That was it. Meant butt, tushy, derriere. She doubled over laughing. She couldn't help it. The sight of composed, can-do Katie, flat on her keister in the middle of the kitchen floor, tickled her funnybone. A few people reached to help her up, but Ali was laughing too hard to be one of them.

Upright, Katie dropped all pretense of control.

"You find this funny? You think this whole disgusting scene is some joke?"

Ali blinked. "No. I'm sorry you fell," she said—and started to laugh all over again.

"You're stoned!" Katie accused her. "I can't believe you! I can't believe you'd do this! Do you even know who these . . . degenerates are?"

Ali stopped laughing. "Please don't call my friends degenerates. Besides, this party is for you, too. It's for everyone in our house."

That didn't placate Katie. "Look at this mess! It's . . . it's . . . a shambles! How could you do this?"

"What crawled up your butt?" Mandy was in Katie's face, shoving a shot glass at her. "Here—have a drink, chill out. It's the Not-Fourth-of-July, f'chrissakes, or are you snooty Bostonians still upset over the tea party?"

Katie looked petrified. Like Mandy might take a swing at her.

"We're having fun," Ali put in. "Really, it's just a party. I was sure I told you about it."

"You didn't, because if you had, I would have made sure Mitch knew. I assume he's not here." Katie's arms were crossed defensively, but Alefiya heard a tremor in her voice, like she was struggling not to cry. Instinct kicked in. Ali sobered up and put her arm around Katie's birdlike shoulders. "Hey, look, I'm really, really sorry. I didn't know it would upset you. I thought I told you, and you were cool with it. If you want, we can tell everyone to leave, okay?"

Katie's lip was trembling now, and Ali tried to shield her from Mandy and the others in the room, now a rapt audience. "So, uh, why don't we go outside, where we can talk? I don't think there's that many people in the back."

Katie took a deep breath; it seemed to calm her. "Forget it. I'll just go to my room—"

"Change into some jeans or something and join the party—I made baked Brie, and spinach dip, and baba ghanoush, if you're hungry."

Katie turned and took a step toward the bedrooms. Ali tapped her shoulder. "Hey, I mean it. I'll chase everyone out if you want me to. "

"Never mind." Katie slumped away, looking defeated.

Ali grabbed a couple of beers and made her way back to the den. If she'd learned anything about Katie, it was this: The girl could, and would, adjust. It'd be fine, and if not? She'd try to help her through whatever had made her such a wreck tonight.

Back on the couch now, she threaded her arm around Jeremy's waist. "Is that your big-deal celebrity photographer friend Mandy's talking to?"

Jeremy craned his neck. "I have no idea who

that dude is. The one I was talking about is over there." He pointed toward the alcove near Mitch's room. "He's hanging with some chick in the T-shirt that says something about men and pain. I don't really want to know!"

Ali lit up. "Harper? Awesome. She's my favorite person here. You've gotta meet her, come on—and you *promised* to introduce your photographer friend to Mandy. Do. Not. Forget. On pain of . . . ah, you've met Mandy!"

Jeremy laughed, and pecked Ali on the cheek. "You're the best, you know that, Leaf?"

She punched him lightly in the stomach. "Don't tell anyone—that's our secret."

Ali was aglow—only partly, she knew, from the pot, and the booze, and her handling of Katie. She was the happiest she'd ever been. As she crossed the room with Jeremy, she felt absolutely dazzled by everyone who'd shown up—admittedly way more than she'd assumed—and still more people were arriving. Everyone seemed to be "kickin' it," as Jeremy would say.

Jeremy made good on his offer to introduce his friends to Mandy. Ali didn't catch all the names and their connections, but she did catch Mandy's megawatt smile. That was the best thing about tonight. Mandy was so desperate for help with her career. Maybe these people could help her, maybe not. But Ali knew that just having a friend, someone who supported Mandy's dreams, might end up being just as good.

"*Hey ya', hey ya'* . . . *shake it like a Polaroid picture* . . . *shake it* . . . *shake it* . . ."

Dutifully, Alefiya shook her booty.

The music rocked. Joss had said they could use his CD collection, and he had everything from Prince to the Beatles, from Outkast to cheesy 70s Bee Gees, who were warbling "You Should be Dancin'"; from the Pixies to the guitar God himself, Jimi Jones. Like the eclectic music, the partiers were this amazing cross-section of sentient beings: people of color, tattooed motorcycle dudes, goth girls, preps, locals, college kids, visitors, just everyone. And all because of her. She'd done this.

"This is ALL YOUR FAULT! You dumb-ass LOSER!"

This time, Katie came out *thundering*. Someone cut the music. Everyone froze.

Ali's jaw clenched, only Katie wasn't bellowing at her, but at . . . Harper?

"You're blaming me?" Harper hissed. "For what, your own stupidity? Give me a break."

"Yes, I'm blaming *you*. For this fucked-up summer," Katie spat. "You're too dumb to even know why."

Jeremy advanced toward them, but Ali put her

arm out to stop him. It wasn't his place to be peace-maker.

"I may not be up to your standards of snottiness, but I do know this," Harper continued. "If you got shafted by some guy tonight, it's your own fault. Memo from the twenty-first century, kitten: Guys are not saviors. You'll just have to buck up and do that yourself."

"*You're* the expert on guys?" Katie trilled. "Oh, that's rich."

Harper folded her arms defensively—as if she intuited what might be coming.

Katie was afire. "Three words, holier-than-thou Harper: pussy trumps poetry. Ask any guy. Maybe if you'd put out, Luke Clearwater wouldn't have kicked you to the curb, and neither of us would be in this shithole!"

"What the hell are you talking about?" Harper shouted.

Katie smirked. "Oh, you didn't know, did you? Your soul mate, Luke, left you for my best friend! Lily McCoy!"

# Katie Kicks Butt, but . . . Harper Self-Destructs, Anyway

"Hey, sweet cheeks, you're lookin' good, know what I'm sayin'? Drink up!" Some random guy trying to sound ghetto was all over Harper, burping vodka fumes in her face. In response, Harper snatched the bottle from him, boozily agreeing, "I *am* lookin' good. I'm *doin'* good. I am doin' grrrr-ate! Just like Kate. Oooops! That rhymed." She giggled and guzzled from the bottle. "Hey! I am a poet. An' don' I freakin' know it!"

She followed with another swallow, only she missed her mouth. Using her arm to wipe the vodka off her chin, she stood on tipsy toes and craned her neck to peer around the room. "Am'int I a poet, Jozz? Hey," she demanded, "wheere's Jozz? Why in't he here?"

Katie felt her cheeks redden. She was beyond mortified. Harper, obviously hammered for the first time, had done a complete 180, trading her patented emo-sarcasm for crude, lewd, loud, and proud. Like she'd channeled Mandy on the sauce. Drunk, Harper was self-destructing.

It was all Katie's fault. She'd had a humiliating, thoroughly heinous day. Her mood—her life!—was plummeting downhill, and she could not stop it. Worse, she'd dragged Harper down with her.

How could she have screamed at Harper like that? In front of a room full of people? She'd never, *ever*, let herself get out of control like that. What was happening to her?

Okay, so during the day she and Brian had run into that heinous Taylor Ambrose from school—who delivered the bulletin that she knew Katie was a counselor. When Brian blabbed that Katie was only working for her mom's charitable organization, Taylor laughed evilly. "Believe that if you want. I hear otherwise."

Katie had been freaked. What did Taylor know, and what would she take back to Boston with her? So far, Katie was pretty sure the indictment against her father had not come down yet. What inside info was Taylor privy to? She could not stop shaking all afternoon, and for the gazillionth time she cursed Lily for not being there, for not having her back.

Brian hadn't pushed for an explanation.

That was because, it turned out, he had other things to push for. He thought going out with her for a month entitled him to "more." Sure, they'd hooked up, fooled around—a lot. But he wanted to go further. Why wouldn't he? He also thought she was twenty (that's what she'd told him), and experienced. He was too well bred to come out and say it, but clearly he wasn't far from accusing her of teasing him.

He'd issued a not-so-veiled ultimatum: "Sleep with me, or I'm moving on."

Katie rejected both scenarios, only she didn't know what to do. So she'd pretended to be offended, and demanded he stop the car right that minute—she wasn't going another mile with him, she'd pouted.

Well, who would've expected he'd do just that, even lean over to open the door so she could get out? She was miles from the house, on four-inch heels, literally being kicked to the curb.

She *assumed* Brian would follow, apologize, and at least drive her back.

He chose "none of the above."

Over an hour later, feet killing, ego crushed, she'd come home to this disaster! What kind of idiot was Ali, anyway? Anyone who ever had a house party knew how this would end. The cops would be called. The last thing she needed was to be caught in some stupid roundup of underage drinkers. If word got out she was living in this dump, she'd be the total laughingstock of Trinity!

She had, as Ali suggested, retreated to her room, only to come upon one couple thrashing around on her bed, and a threesome on Harper's side of the room.

Shit! (Without parentheses!)

If Lily were here, none of this would be happening. If Lily were here, she'd help her handle Brian (from whom at least she'd managed to snare some cash: some he willingly lent her, some he didn't know about). Lily would have advice; they'd have figured this thing out together, the way they always did.

It was all Harper's fault that Lily wasn't here. Harper's own fault that Luke had dumped her and taken up with Lily; Harper's fault that a hundred strangers were tearing apart her house, that she had nowhere to turn, no one to turn to.

That she didn't know what to do.

She'd lost it. And by doing so, she set in motion a total disaster. After the runaway words had sped from her mouth, they'd crashed through Harper's chest, piercing the girl's heart. Ali—who else?—had rushed to her, and soon Jeremy, a bunch of other people, and even Mandy had joined in, helping to dull Harper's pain with alcohol. Oodles of booze.

At first, Katie had rushed outside, panting—the verbal assault had taken the wind out of her—then forced herself to walk the streets, take deep breaths, calm down, and assess. What she'd just done to Harper? It was the most hurtful thing she'd ever done to anyone (to their face, that is). She'd just made innocent Harper pay for Lily's betrayal.

That realization finally forced her back to the party. At the very least, she would apologize. At most, she thought, surveying the scene now, she'd try to save Harper from herself.

Harper wasn't going to make it easy.

Katie watched helplessly as Harper, arms swaying in the air now, wove suggestively through the room, purposely bumping into as many boys as she could, like a Missy Elliot backup dancer: *"Work it, now reverse it, put my thing down, and reverse it . . ."* She accosted Sharif, who'd been dancing with Lisa. Harper shouted above the music, "Are you dancing, or having a seizure?"

Then, she grabbed him and planted a full openmouthed kiss, with obvious tongue, on his surprised lips. Further down the sinkhole of bad behavior, Harper leered at a shocked Lisa. "You should thank me. 'Cause he'll leave you, just like that." She punctuated by snapping her fingers, and moving on.

Katie tried to grab her, but Harper wasn't having it. "Unhand me, Princess Poopypants!" she yelled, flouncing away, bumping into more guys and rapping loudly, *"Keep ya' eyes on my bomp-a-bomp-bomp."*

"Harper, you need to come with me!" Katie's pleas were drowned out as Harper blurted, "Let's play charades!" as she bounded into the kitchen, grabbed the scissors, and cut her T-shirt around the collar, then pulled it over one shoulder, doing the worst *Fame* impression ever, singing at the top of her lungs. *"I'm gonna live forever, baby remember my name! Fame!"*

Katie needed help. Ali—or even Mandy, at this point. But at the moment, she could find neither. She pushed through the throng, some clapping and encouraging Harper, others caught up in drinking, dancing, and canoodling, and oh God, Katie saw two people with their noses to the kitchen counter, sniffing. She went back into the living room, just in time to catch Mandy's backside as the house skank headed up the stairs, arm in arm with the guy she'd been circling.

"Mandy!" Katie called out. "Wait, I need you."

Mandy stopped, turned, and grinned cruelly at her. "No, you don't. You're Katie-I'm-So-Above-It-All Charlesworth, you don't need anyone."

Katie turned on her heel and redoubled her efforts to unearth Ali. But when she found her, Ali was sitting on the floor, with Clarence in her lap.

She'd tied her red, white, and blue do-rag around the ferret and was singing "America the Beautiful" to him, backed up by Jeremy, Sharif, and Lisa.

Okay, she'd do this herself, physically remove Harper from the house. But when she turned around, the way was blocked: A circle three people deep had formed around the middle of the den, where Harper had decided that since charades wasn't working, a new game was called for. She'd run down the steps leading to the basement and had come upstairs with a board game.

Twister.

"Let's get naked and play!" Her shouts were greeted with hoots, woo-hoos, and squeals.

Which Harper took as a cue to remove her T-shirt. Instantly, she was joined by dozens of happy partyers. Someone cranked the music up louder; another shouted, "Lime shots here! Come 'n' get them!"

The game had begun, and unsurprisingly, got out of control quickly. Harper's leg wound around a guy's, and they fell. Others got to the floor to help them up. In the process, someone opened Harper's jeans—aided and abetted by another guy, who pulled them down.

She protested incoherently. "Hey, whatcha doin'? I wuzzin' out."

"Yo, this isn't strip poker, sweetcheeks, it's naked

Twister! You said so y'self! We're just helpin' ya get nekkid!"

Katie panicked. She was responsible for this and she had to fix it, with or without anyone's help. But just then, her stomach lurched. Whirring sirens screamed up the block. Flashing red strobe lights lit the living room.

The cops.

Katie raced into serious action. Her four-inch heels good for something, she kicked and punched and bit, and grabbed handfuls of hair to get to Harper, who, by that time, was pinned on the floor, a dozen guys pawing her. Katie dove on top of them, and with all her strength, managed to get most of the guys off her. Katie grabbed Harper's hands, and—now, finally, with Jeremy's help—pulled her upright. Together, they tried to get her outside, but Harper wasn't having it. Dazed and confused, but conscious enough to try and get away from Katie, she broke loose. At that second, the door flew open. Harper lunged into the arms of the first guy through the door.

And promptly threw up all over him.

# Hangovers, Heroes, and Hope

### *Joss*

Joss moved stealthily and swiftly. Barely one step ahead of the sirens, he flew into the house, tossed the hurling, half-dressed Harper over his shoulder, and ran. He dodged out the back door, betting the cops wouldn't bother to come after him. Breaking up house parties packed with underage kids drinking and doping had to be routine for them. They'd haul in a bunch of them and call it a night. He didn't worry for Katie and Mandy; they were survivors. They'd get out.

Ali was most likely to offer herself up on the altar of confession, in a backward attempt to prevent trouble for the others. He could only hope someone had talked better sense into her. Otherwise, dude, she'd be in for one hell of a sobering night. Ali had mentioned something about a party, but it hadn't really registered. In her spacey way, she said a lot of things. Didn't mean she'd actually do it. Make that, overdo it.

This was a bad scene; yet, running down the beach, a heady sense of adventure filled him, as if eluding the fuzz with a helplessly hammered chick was something he did all the time. It was like James Bond, only he was the antihero. For the first time since he'd ditched his life of privilege, he wasn't just free, he felt unshackled.

If only he could stop the spinning wheels in his head. He knew what would happen next. After the roundup, after parents had been notified, and some kids had spent the night in the clink, the police would find the person whose name was on the lease.

That would suck. Mitch, the poor slob, would be blindsided, and since he was over twenty-one, held accountable. Joss was sorely tempted to intervene. All he had to do was make one call, and the whole incident would be erased, like it'd never happened. That, however, meant calling his father, using his family connections. And he'd cut those ties, man.

Harper, who'd stopped upchucking, now kicked and punched him. "Put me down!" she managed to belch out.

Turning to be sure they hadn't been followed, Joss slowed enough to let Harper slide off him. He didn't free her completely, though. He kept a grip on her slender wrists so she wouldn't run off.

"Let me go!" she cried, fighting him, pulling away.

"It's okay, it's okay, it's gonna be okay," he said soothingly.

Then Harper looked up at him, and he wanted to die.

What had happened to her? She was ravaged. Her innocent, beautiful face was stained, scratched, smeared; her hair stuck in clumps to her wet cheeks. Her eyes were red and puffy. Were those bruises on her neck—or maybe hickeys? It has hard to tell in the dark. Her bra hung off her shoulder; her pants were down around her ankles. Joss hoped they'd fallen while they were running. He didn't want to even think of the alt-scenario, that they'd been removed during the party.

His heart ached as he folded her into his arms and kissed the top of her head. "Let's go over to the water, get washed up a little. Okay? It'll be all right, little one, I promise."

In his entire life, Joss had never welshed on a promise.

For once, he was glad the bartending gig forced him to wear a jacket over his shirt. He'd need both.

Peeling them off, he soaked his soiled shirt in the surf and used it as towel, cleansing Harper's face, arms, and neck. Eventually, she stopped fighting him, refastened her bra, closed her trousers, and accepted his jacket as cover-up. She wrapped it tightly around herself. She looked like a wet, bedraggled wire-haired terrier, all big, baleful eyes. And Joss wanted to hold her, to tell her she could confide in him, that he could make it go away. He knew better than to say, or do, anything. It would be up to Harper to tell him what had happened—if she ever wanted to.

### KATIE

Katie had escaped the roundup by tailing Joss out the back door, then hiding behind the fence, watching others pour out the house. Only the first wave had managed to avoid capture. The two squad cars on the scene had apparently called for backup and, within five minutes, enough cops were at 345 Cranberry Lane to escort dozens upon dozens of party goers into the paddy wagon and off to the precinct.

No way could Katie allow herself to be caught, even if only to be let go a few hours later. From sporadic e-mails back and forth to her parents, she knew nothing had gone down yet—they were on their cruise, all was well, and they assumed she and Lily were ensconced in the McCoy mansion in

Chatham. The FBI had not come calling on the Charlesworths, nor would anyone be looking for her yet. Even though Taylor Ambrose might have some intel about her working at a drone job, Katie needed to be under the radar until she could figure out a scheme.

Katie had waited a good half hour after all the squad cars had gone before slipping back inside. So far as she could tell, she was alone.

The place was trashed. Bottles, butts, and smashed glass littered the living room floor. Lamps had been kicked, or had fallen over; two of the couches bore the scars of cigarette burns. And one thought pounded at her: Lily.

If Lily were here, Katie wouldn't be.

If Lily were here, Katie'd never have driven a stake into poor Harper's heart.

If Lily were here, Katie wouldn't be scared shitless.

Just then, something skittered across the floor and Katie jumped, screaming. Clarence. The stupid ferret—dragging the do-rag on his foot—had smelled food and had scampered across the room to feast on it. Slowly, Katie's heart settled back to normal.

Sure that the kitchen was in worse shape than the living room, she didn't even want to check it out. She needed to do something, call someone. She found her cell phone and dialed Mitch.

## *MITCH*

It was nearing dawn when Mitch, tossing and turning on the couch in Leonora's den, got Katie's panicked call. He was only surprised it hadn't happened sooner. Of course there'd be a party—he was a veteran of too many summer shares to know it was inevitable. Didn't matter what rule he imposed. It was like the Cape Cod fog, or the windswept beaches, its own force of nature during a summer in a house shared by six young strangers. This time, he'd likely be held accountable since his name was on the lease. But it was useless to stress. Until the cops came for him, there was a ton of work to be done.

He took charge, like always, and without whining, placing blame, blowing a gasket, or otherwise giving in to his emotions, Mitch methodically got everyone aboard the cleanup train. He sent Joss to the twenty-four-hour Meijers in Centerville for mops, buckets, industrial-size garbage bags, and other supplies. He taught Katie how to use a vacuum cleaner, and after calming a guilt-ridden Ali, set her to scouring the kitchen. "Go slowly and carefully," he cautioned the whimpering girl.

Then he rolled up his sleeves. Until Joss got back, the heavy lifting was his alone. Of the two housemates not participating, his concern was only for one. Not Mandy. In the beginning of the summer, at his sister Beverly's suggestion, he'd programmed his cell phone number into her Nokia. Since she hadn't called, he assumed she wasn't in police custody—nor was she alone.

He was nervous about Harper, who, despite her stinging sarcasm, he'd become really fond of. He wondered what had caused her to get so drunk, so out of control. Joss, who'd rescued her, claimed not to know.

Mitch believed the guy. His suspicions lay with Katie and Ali. He was sure something had precipitated it, and they knew what it was. But no one was saying. As he hoisted the remains of another smashed lamp into a black garbage bag, he rewound to the real reason for his own quiet freak-out.

Leonora hadn't bailed on him, as he'd feared. She'd been ready, on time, when he came to pick her up—Lee, the girl who always kept him waiting. Maybe that should've been his first clue. The rest of the evening she'd been, what? Contrite? Wary? Jittery? Too quick to laugh at his seriously lame jokes. Too chatty over dinner, too interested—if that were even possible—as he blathered about his tennis clients at the Chelsea House, listening without hearing. She was flushed, fluttery, and kept looking at him weirdly—guiltily, even. As if she was searching his face for a clue to something. But what? That he loved her? That he wanted to spend the rest of his life with her? She knew all that.

Her bizarre behavior made him squirm. He kept asking if anything was wrong. After saying no several times, she asked, carefully, "Should there be? I mean . . . is there something you think . . . ?" She'd trailed off.

After dinner, they'd gone back to her parents' house, empty for the weekend. He didn't know what was bothering her, but he thought he knew how to make it better. Mitch had gotten romantic, drawn her into his arms, and begun kissing her in that way—their way, the way that usually led to love-making.

Not so much. "Mitch," she'd murmured, pulling away. "I can't. Stop."

"But we're finally alone," he'd countered, hurt and surprised.

She hung her head, then looked up at him with pursed lips. "I know. But . . . I just . . . I'd rather not. Not tonight."

Scared, Mitch coaxed: "Baby, we've barely seen each other. We've waited so long to be alone together. What's wrong? Whatever it is, I can fix it. You know that."

Leonora began to sob. "I'm sorry, Mitch. I'm so, so sorry."

He never did find out what she was sorry about.

She fled into her room and locked the door. He lay on the couch. And then Katie called.

### *HARPER*

Harper awoke the next morning sick to her stomach. Her head killed, her body throbbed and ached. But there was something more, something else that felt sour, and painful. It had happened last night, during the party. But what was it? She tried to sit up, but her head was too heavy for her body. She couldn't raise it off the pillow.

Her cell phone rang—damn, had she set it on "Blast"? Without checking the caller ID, she managed to reach out and hit the "Silence" button. That movement was all it took to set her stomach to churning, and she knew she'd better move. Fast.

Harper barely made it to the bathroom. After washing herself off, she braved the mirror—which set her stomach in motion again, forcing her once again to kneel by the toilet and heave. When she felt sure there was nothing left inside her, she brushed her teeth and washed up again. Suddenly, the freakin' roar of a motorcycle engine revved up right outside the bathroom. What the—?

She flung the door open.

There was Katie, cute-as-you-please, running a vacuum cleaner along the hallway.

Snap! Everything came back to her, played out in her head like a video set on rewind. She saw the shock in her own eyes, felt the horrible hurt as Katie spat that vile thing about pussy trumping poetry. She saw her "friends," Ali and company, rush to her; remembered the metallic taste of the tequila, hot down her throat, drink after drink until it obliterated everything. All she remembered from the devastating humiliation of what had happened afterward was a purple-and-white-striped shirt that Joss had used to clean her up, his warm jacket, his pitying face.

"Harper, are you okay?" Katie asked tremulously. "I feel so awful, I never meant—"

Oh, she'd meant it all right. Every sickening word of it. That Luke had dumped Harper because he wanted to have sex with someone else. Worse, that someone else turned out to be Katie's best friend, Lily McCoy, a stupid, superficial, self-absorbed slut.

Because of Luke, Lily had abandoned Katie—left her stranded this summer.

Because of Luke, Harper had abandoned Boston—and ended up stranded with devious, mean Katie this summer.

It really sucks when you're the *I* in irony.

Harper got right in Katie's face. The only thing left inside her was bile; she managed to spit it at Katie.

### *MANDY*

Mandy was p.o.'ed. Why was everyone in the house so freaked? By the time she returned on Monday morning, the place was sparkling. Spanking clean; looked better than it ever had. The floors shined, the counters gleamed; the rugs had been shampooed—dude, even the bathrooms had been good and disinfected. Place looked better than when they'd moved in, f'crissakes.

She expected no less of Saint Mitch, who was born with a PhD in TCB: taking care of business. Even as a kid, he was all Mr. Responsible. For his sister, Beverly, his mother, Dora, and sometimes, going way back, for Sarah herself.

So a bunch of random rich kids had gotten arrested. Big deal. Not one of *them* had. As far as she could tell, Ali, Katie, and Harper had eluded the cops. Joss hadn't even been there.

As for Mitch, guess what? Queen Leonora's well-connected daddy had come to the rescue. It just proved it was all who you know, not what you know. Daddy Leonora had made a call to the Hyannis police, and poof! No arrest, no record for Mitchell Considine. Homeboy was off the hook.

So what was with the scowling, the stomping around, the flying accusations, and, from Mitch to her, the scolding. All she'd done was enjoy herself, accent on the j-o-y. She'd had a blast at the party, and thanks to the fat cow Ali, had been introduced to the man of her dreams: one Timothy Johnson—Timmy-Cakes, to her—who ran with the showbiz crowd; worked as a best boy on movies and TV shows filmed on the Cape. Who, ta *da!*, right now, after their weekend of fun, fun, fun, was back on the job with *Skinny Dipping*, the movie starring Jude Law and Scarlett Johannson, being filmed on Martha's Vineyard.

Tim knew *everyone*. He lived right here in Hyannis—partied with the Kennedys, even—but, more important, stud-boy was tight with directors, agents, producers. He hadn't introduced her to anyone yet; Mandy was working on it, using her personal powers of persuasion. Soon, he'd be at her beck and call and she'd be on her way. Woofuckin'-hoo! Mandy was feeling so generous, she even resolved to clean the frickin' bathroom next time it was her turn.

**14**

Cape Cod

# *Heal, Harper, Heal!*

Harper removed the plastic bowl from the fridge, gently lifted the lid, and sniffed. Ewww. Nooo, tabouli salad did not last forever, contrary to popular myth. Holding it at arm's length, she dumped the whole concoction in the garbage, plastic container and all. Bad Harper, she chastised herself for her un-eco (antirecyclable) action. She couldn't drum up enough feeling to care. She hunted through the messy cabinet and, finding a bag of wheat pasta, put up a pot of water to boil.

It was around seven on Saturday night, and, clad in her worn flannel pj's, she'd decided to scrounge up some dinner and curl up with her journal, fairly sure she had the place to herself.

Katie, who'd rebounded seamlessly from the

Brian boot-off—*quelle* shockeroo!—had claimed her next victim. Nate Graham was another young, rich, and restless hotel guest. Although, Harper thought, astoundingly raffish for conservo-Barbie. But they'd been out every night this week, including tonight. Nate and Kate. Out on a date. Flirt, Katie, flirt. Retch, Harper, retch.

To be sure, her righteous roommate kept trying to apologize for her vicious, humiliating outburst during the party. But ya know what, Harper thought, pouring Katie's beloved orange juice down the drain—oooh, too bad, all gone—screw her. Except when a verbal exchange was absolutely necessary—mostly at camp—she was all stony silence toward Katie.

Harper ripped open the bag of pasta and dumped it into the now boiling water. She found the wooden spoon in the sink, rinsed it, and began stirring.

The post-party doldrums pervaded the house; everyone was either "in a mood" or not around. Even happy-go-slobby Ali was mopey, blaming herself for the disastrous turn the night had taken. Her friends, especially Jeremy—who was definitely into her—were taking her out tonight to lift her spirits.

Mandy pretty much slept the days away, and never alone. The guy she'd attached herself to at the party seemed to have moved into her room.

Just as Mitch, for all intents and purposes, had practically moved out. His gig at Chelsea House, he'd explained, had gotten more intense: He was now giving weekend and evening tennis lessons. After work, he generally saw Leonora, running every time she snapped her betraying bling-fingers.

How could Mitch not see what was going on? She wanted to shake him. Guilt, guilt, guilt! It was out of guilt! she wanted to scream at Mitch. Your beloved is sleeping with someone else, someone married! And dig, no doubt girlfriend was walking on eggshells, wondering if Harper would tell. But Harper hadn't had the heart.

But how blind could Mitch be?

How blind had she been? She never saw Luke's betrayal coming either. Had no clue he'd leave her for "Katie-Lite": that thimble-brained slut, Lily.

That arsenic-laced diatribe Katie had thrown about "putting out"? It was just wrong. Luke wasn't like other guys. That's why she'd fallen for him. They'd opened up to each other in ways far deeper than sex. Luke had said so!

Whatever. Harper lifted her chin. Making the same mistake twice was not gonna happen.

"Harper . . . ?"

She whirled. Joss was pointing at the stove.

Joss. Oh God, she'd been avoiding him. What was he doing here? He was supposed to be at work.

"Turn the water off. You're boiling over."

"I am?" Harper repeated, confused. She looked at the stove. "Crap-damnit!" Bubbling waves of white-hot pasta foam erupted like lava spilling from mini-volcanoes, covering the pot, seeping into the burner, over the counter, heading for the floor.

She quickly killed the heat just as Joss went to remove the pot from the stove.

"Don't!" Harper grabbed his arm to stop him. "You'll get burned. Wait—I'll get a dish towel."

Chagrined, he gave her a loopy smile. "Yeah. Good idea."

Harper blushed, and got to work mopping the mess of soggy spaghetti and water. She didn't know if she was more embarrassed or ashamed. Twice now, Joss had seen her make a fool of herself. Once, she'd been half naked. He'd been gentleman enough to not bring it up. She'd been the coward— never even thanked him.

"Lucky for me you're here," she managed, furiously sponging off the stovetop. "How come you're not at work?"

"Donated my shift to another bartender—guy's desperate for dough." Joss handed her a roll of paper towels. "Here, use this. I'll get the floor."

"Thanks," Harper murmured. She wanted to say, "For everything, for saving me from further humiliation." But the words didn't come.

"Well," Joss mused as he wiped up, "hope you weren't jonesing for pasta. This dinner is beyond saving."

"No big," she said. Then her stomach growled. Loudly.

Josh laughed. "Hey look, I got the night off. So why don't we just chuck it . . . as it were . . . go out to dinner instead?"

Harper shook her head, more adamantly than she'd meant. "No! I mean, thanks and all, but . . ."

"But what? I know this place, you'll dig it—a real Cape Cod experience, on the beach up in Wellfleet. Been there?"

"I'm a vegetarian." And she'd blurted that, why, exactly?

"Then don't get a hamburger. Chill, it's just dinner."

It wasn't. Just dinner, that is.

It was the best time Harper'd had in weeks! Joss had nailed it. The Beachcomber was her kind of place: kick back, outdoor, a bar-restaurant, with an awesome view. It was snuggled atop a dune, overlooking a wide, pristine beach. They got there just at sunset. The sand seemed to be bathed in hues of rust, orange, red-clay; and the ocean, a dark navy.

The Beachcomber wasn't visible from the road; you had to know about it. Hence, the place was filled with locals: a homey mix of singles, couples, families, in their faded denims, Old Navy tees, sandals, and flip-flops. Not a Katie-type in sight. Harper and Joss bypassed the green-and-white-awninged bar, and settled at one of the few tables still empty.

"This place has been here for decades," Joss told her. "It's famous for its authentic Cape Cod oysters, and after dark, it's a big music scene. Concerts on the beach: jazz, rock, punk, reggae—you name it. Everyone's played the Beachcomber, from Dylan, back in the day, to Dave Matthews."

"You've been here before," Harper noted.

"Once—which makes me qualified to order for both of us."

Harper couldn't suppress a grin. Joss was so sure of himself, he just took over. He'd picked the place, driven them here in his cute rented convertible—he'd even maneuvered their seats so they'd both be facing the ocean. Was it because he was older—at least twenty-one, she calculated—or was he hard-wired that way? Both, she thought.

"We'll have a dozen bluepoint oysters on the half shell to start," he told the waiter, "a mountain of your greasiest onion rings, and a couple of beers." He turned to Harper. "Uh, unless you don't want beer?"

"Sounds like it's part of the oyster/onion ring Cape experience."

Joss conceded, "It is. You kind of have to."

"Then I kind of want to," she said with a real smile.

To the waiter, Joss joked, "The lady is an oyster virgin, so we'll start her on the classic, then build to more exotic varied types. If she's up to it, that is." He winked.

Harper leaned back, clasped her hands behind her head, put her feet up on the extra chair. "How'd you know I've never had oysters?"

"Just a guess. Not many neighborhood hangouts in Boston—or New York—that serve 'em. It's not like HoJo's fried clams, or The Original Ray's Pizza, if you know what I mean."

"What do they taste like?" Harper was suddenly hyperaware that Joss was sitting really close to her.

He ran his fingers through his long curls. "Hard to describe. I think you're just gonna have to decide for yourself."

When their order arrived, Harper was about to decide to order something else. Oysters weren't much for eye appeal. She knew what they were: plump bivalves—muscles, really—in simple juice. Only they looked like pearly gray lumps of quivering phlegm-y slime, set in a ragged shell. Dude, it looked like something you'd send flying *out* your throat, not down it. Not that Harper would dare say that.

She didn't have to.

"Not much of a poker face, are you?" Joss grinned. "Don't be grossed out. Here, I'll show you how it's done."

Harper watched, transfixed, as Joss demonstrated. "First, we dab a little cocktail sauce just here." He spooned a drop of the red sauce onto the fat middle of the oyster, then, with his thumb and forefinger, lifted the ringed shell. "You hoist it up to your lips, open your mouth, stick your tongue out, tip your chin up . . . and let it slide down your throat. Hmmm . . ." He winked at her and took a slug of beer.

"I don't know . . ." Harper was dubious. What if she choked on the thing? What if it got stuck in her throat?

"Don't be a wuss," Joss needled good-naturedly. "Nobody respects a wuss."

"A wuss? Did you just call me a wuss?" Harper attacked the oyster, drowning it first in cocktail sauce. She shut her eyes—and just did it. The slippery *thing* slid down, sort of like a log flume ride. She tasted mainly the cocktail sauce—that was a relief!

"Beer chaser," Joss advised, handing her a bottle. "Next time, slow down so you can actually savor it. By the way, chewing is acceptable too."

Harper reached for a comeback, only seeing

herself—the fading sun glinting off her blond streaks, the mile-wide smile, her dimples—in the mirror of Joss's swimming-pool-blue eyes, she forgot what it was. Then she noticed what he was wearing. A purple-and-white-striped button-down beneath his jacket. "That's not the shirt—"

"You threw up all over?" He finished her sentence with a laugh. "Nah, that one didn't make it."

The elephant dropped onto the table. Time to do the right thing. Haltingly, Harper did. "About that night . . . I'm so very sorry, so ashamed, I don't usually—"

"Get hammered and hurl over the first guy who comes into the room?"

Harper fixed her gaze straight ahead, to the line where the water met the sky: the horizon. A lone boat tossed on the choppy water, and a lone tear wiggled its way down her cheek.

Joss leaned over and pulled her to him. "I'm sorry, I didn't mean to trivialize it. I figured something monumental must have happened."

"You could say that," Harper whispered, tempted to let herself go, lean into his chest.

"You don't owe me an explanation," Joss said sincerely. "It's cool, really, we're good."

Harper swallowed and pulled away. "Katie got in my face with some nasty stuff. I reacted badly."

If Joss knew more—and by this time, he probably did—he didn't let on. He did empathize, though.

"I get it. I'm slow to burn, but push my buttons, and man, all bets are off. Back in high school, this jerk ripped into me, talked real trash about my dad cheating on my mom. I didn't even know I had it in me, I just hauled off and dropped him."

Harper quipped, "Put the 'fist' in pacifist, did you?"

"Oh, yeah. Didn't go unnoticed. Our school was right across the street from the police precinct. New York's finest earned their rep that day."

Harper lit up. Joss had just said the magic words: "New York."

# Katie Whispers in the Wind

Had Harper or Joss been looking out at the water as keenly as they were eyeing each other, they might've spotted a small luxury yacht called *Lady Blue* cruising Cape Cod Bay. But by the time Nathan Graham's family-owned ferry passed by the Wellfleet inlet, the two were animatedly comparing experiences in New York and having an oyster eat-off.

It was just around 9:30 that night, and Katie stood at the railing, Nate's arms locked around her. She took in the shoreline, dotted with restaurants, souvenir shops, surf shacks, beaches. Her eye settled on a cute place with a green-and-white-striped awning, tables situated just at the top of a dune. How sweet is that? she thought, never guessing that Harper and Joss were sitting there. Nate leaned in and nuzzled her neck. "You cold, cupcake?"

Katie burrowed into him. "Not anymore."

"Mmmm, 'cause we can go inside the cabin any-time you want," her date pointed out, in that sweetly suggestive way of his.

"I like being out on the open water, under the moonlit sky," Katie replied. "There's something so romantic about it, like possibilities are limitless."

She'd gotten romantic with Nate Graham in record time, even for her. But what choice had she had? Brian had bruised her ego, rushed her, all before she'd had a chance to ask him for help.

She could try again. Brian had called repeatedly, tried to woo his way back into her good graces. Was it worth it? Though she'd met Brian and Nate the same day, Katie had chosen Brian first because he seemed like the better bet. Brainy, brawny, an old-money blue blood. The type she understood, and thought she could manipulate.

But, no—Katie's mind was made up. Brian's ship had sailed.

Nate, though he'd demonstrated squeal appeal for her prepubescent campers, had stalled at number two, because he wasn't really Katie's type. Short and wiry with blond bed-head spikes, Nate had grown up here on the Cape, vaulted from high school straight into the family business, which was boating.

His family came by its money via the fleet of

ferries they owned and operated all over New England, an empire that had started with Nate's great-granddad and continued to flourish under the helm of his parents, himself, and his siblings. They had docks at Hyannis, Provincetown, Wellfleet, and Barnstable Harbor and did healthy business taking tourists to and from Martha's Vineyard, Nantucket, and, of course, on scenic cruises around the Cape itself.

The vessels reserved for the family's personal use went beyond ferries to sailboats, skiffs, schooners, motorboats, yachts—all fully staffed. There was, Katie quickly calculated, quite a cache of cash at Nate's disposal. He'd do quite nicely at the keeping-up-appearances game. Aside from that, he really was a nice guy.

"Sure you want to stay outside?" Nate asked. "I think we can be pretty romantic if we go inside."

"In a little while," Katie answered. "Let's go around the tip of the Cape one more time, okay? I want to see Provincetown again."

"If that'll make you happy, Katie," Nate said, suddenly serious. "You know, don't you, you're the kind of girl a guy would anything for. Why you're wasting your time with me, that's the mystery."

Katie softened. "You're sweet, you know, really sweet. Hey, could you bring me another drink? A wine spritzer, or just sparkling water, either one."

"Hi-yi, Captain." Nate gave her a mock salute.

"But there'll be a charge for that. You have to pay in advance."

Katie threw her arms around his neck and pressed herself to him. "What's the toll?" she asked coyly.

"I'm thinking one of your special sweet kisses should do it," he murmured.

"And I'm thinking I can do better than that," she told him, moving her hand down his back, sliding it under the waistband of his briefs. It was a promise of more to come, though she felt secure that Nate, unlike Brian, would not push her. This beau was younger, just eighteen to Brian's twenty-two. *Vive la différence!* She didn't have to pretend to know more than she did, to have experienced more than she had.

Maybe she would sleep with him, and maybe even confide in him. Maybe Nathan Graham would give her the life raft she longed for, something for her to hold on to, to save her from drowning in disgrace along with her family.

Or maybe not. She wasn't lying when she told Nate how much she loved being out on the open water, seeing the world from the sanctuary of a private yacht. Maybe she wouldn't think about the end of the summer.

But as she waited for Nate to return, Katie stood perfectly still at the railing, letting the ocean breeze blow her long hair back. "What's gonna happen to me?" she wondered, whispering into the wind.

# Mitch and Mandy Take It Sweet and Sour

"Hey, Mandy, hold up a minute." Mitch stopped her as she sashayed out of the house, her stilettos clicking.

She waved at him. "No time, chico. My ride's almost here."

It was just past 10 p.m. on Saturday night. Both had been out all day, only returning to the cottage for a quick shower before heading out again for the night. Mitch, who'd worked late, was meeting up with Leonora, hoping to finally understand what was tearing his beloved apart. By now, he'd diagnosed severe unhappiness in his girl. But if he didn't know the cause, he had no hope of fixing it.

He wasn't sure what Mandy was up to, only that he didn't like it. Admittedly, he hadn't seen a lot of her post-party, but to his eyes, she looked more and more like a cheap . . . you-know-what . . . every day. Tonight, she'd squeezed herself into some way-too-low, too-tight tank top that practically pushed her boobs up to her chin.

"Make some time," he urged. "Five minutes—you can spare that much for an old friend, can't you?"

Mandy snapped her gum and winked at him. "Oh, Mitchell, you always did have a way of persuading the girls. Hang tight." She flipped open her cell phone, hit speed dial, and after a few seconds, said, "Hi, Timmy-cakes—yeah, it's *moi*. I'm running a little late. Be ready in ten minutes." After listening for a second, she added, "I'm always worth the wait, aren't I?"

Suddenly feeling like an eavesdropper, Mitch cleared his throat. "Sounds like someone you care about. I'm happy for you."

She regarded him warily. "Care about? Yeah, I'm a regular Care Bear. Especially tonight, since he's taking me to the *Skinny Dipping* set!"

"The *Skinny Dipping* set?"

"Yeah, that new movie—haven'tcha heard about it? It's got Jude Law, been filming over on Martha's Vineyard. Timmy's the best boy."

Best boy? Mitch scratched his chin. He'd never heard Mandy refer to anyone that way.

She threw her head back and laughed. A cascade of brassy red curls caught his eye, and instantly took him back to the time when those ringlets were strawberry-blond pigtails, and this overly made-up woman a chubby, bright-eyed girl named Sarah.

"You have no idea what I'm talkin' about, do you, Mitchell? You don't know movie-speak."

He flushed. "Educate me."

A "best boy" described Timmy's job, not Mandy's feelings about him. Those pretty much began and ended with his contacts. "Timmy's friend is the still photographer on the set. D'ya know what that means?

"Not the cameraman, but the guy who takes pictures of the actors?" Mitch guessed.

"A-plus for Saint Mitchell," Mandy said without sarcasm. "So his name is Joe Lester, and after they wrap tonight, Tim's gonna introduce me. And," she continued, her spirits high, "if all goes well, he's gonna book time for my photo session. My first professional photo session. Whatcha think—Mandy's not doin' too bad for herself. A fat girl from the projects?"

Mitch had a soft spot for that twinkle in her eye. It had always attracted him, made him believe in her, even though he had no real reason to. The odds of Mandy Starr—née Sarah Riley—of the downtrodden Dorchester Housing Projects becoming a movie star were pretty much slim, and none.

Yet still she believed in herself. Mitch couldn't find it in himself to contradict her.

"So what'd ya want to talk to me about?" Mandy asked.

Mitch scratched his head again, uncomfortable. "Well, it's . . . I don't know. That guy, that Tim. He's been spending an awful lot of time here."

"Your point?" The twinkle in Mandy's eye had disappeared.

"Well, I just mean, how well do you even know him? Is he trustworthy?"

She bristled. "How well does anybody know anyone? As far as you or anyone in this house is concerned, he's my boyfriend. That's all you need to know. End of story."

"Whoa, slow down, Mandy. I'm just asking a question. I see him—we all do—hanging out here even when you're at work. And I just want to make sure you're okay with that."

"Just spit it out Mitch, okay? You think, what, he's gonna rape and pillage if I'm not around to keep an eye on him? Have you had this finger-wagging scolding with Alefyia? She brings home anything that isn't nailed down."

Mitch frowned. This was not going the way he'd hoped. "My concern isn't for the house. It's for you. I don't want to see you being used. Or getting hurt." There, he'd said it.

The hint of a smile returned to her freckled face. Tenderly, Mandy cupped his chin. "We're not in Dorchester anymore, Mitch. You're not the cops and you don't have to protect me anymore. We've both come a long, long way. So trust me, okay?"

Impulsively, he hugged her. "Take care of yourself, Sarah."

She pulled away. "Right back atcha, Mitchell. Sometimes I think it's you who needs taking care of."

Mandy always did have good gut instincts. Mitch was very not okay. And he could not, for the life of him, figure out why. Okay, the summer had gotten off to a shaky start, but he was proud of the way he'd adjusted, put together the house share. That was something. It showed versatility, adapting to adversity. It showed he was resilient, strong, a leader.

They were just the attributes a girl like Leonora admired, needed, wanted. The qualities that would make him the husband she deserved, the father of her children, if all went well.

And the fact that he loved her desperately, would do anything for her, forgive anything. Didn't that count? So what had changed?

The night of the party, he'd called Leonora—not to ask for her father's help. Anything but. He was his own man, and if he had to be held accountable for the damage, so be it. At least no one had been injured, or gotten really sick or anything. When Leonora immediately offered to have her father call the county police commissioner, he told her it wasn't necessary. But she kept pressing, insisting she let Mr. Quivvers help. And Mitch interpreted: Leonora wouldn't want her future husband to have a black mark on his record. Only because it meant she still loved him, still cared about their future together, had he swallowed his pride and allowed himself the benefit of Lee's well-connected dad. For her sake.

It hadn't changed Lee's attitude toward him. Still, she ran hot and cold, overly solicitous one minute, the next, pushing him away. He hadn't told any of the house share people about his Lee issues. Which made it all the weirder that Harper kept obliquely referring to it, slipping in snide comments like, "Have you ever considered you'd be better off without Leonora? Maybe you should rethink this. Relationships all go sour."

Inserting herself in his love life was so inappropriate, Mitch reminded her, sometimes really angrily. For a microsecond he wondered if she was into him, and therefore jealous? But any nincompoop could see how she looked at Joss. Nah, not jealousy. Then what? From what he'd gathered, Harper's meltdown at the party had something to do with a cutting remark from Katie. About a boy who'd obviously broken Harper's heart. So maybe that was it.

What ate at him wasn't Harper, though. It was just now, the look in Mandy's eye when she told him to take care. Was there something she intuited he should be mindful of?

Mitch finished shaving, put on a clean shirt, khakis, and Docksiders, and banished Mandy from his mind. He checked beneath his mattress for the envelope and carefully counted. The engagement ring fund was now just past the $5,000 mark. Just another few weeks, that was all he needed. Once she saw that sparkler, dude, he was there. Reassured, Mitch locked up. He resolved to redouble his efforts with Lee, no matter what it took.

# Harper and Joss: Treble in Paradise

"Rockin' night!" Joss exclaimed, looking up at the sky. He breathed in deeply: The stars winked at him, the salt air filled with heady promise. And all he wanted was for the night not to end. He'd just treated Harper to her first authentic Cape Cod experience: oysters, onion rings, and beer, sucking in the sea breeze, gazing out at the ocean. It'd been awesome. Once they got past her stammering apologies-slash-gratitude about the party; once he finally told her, yeah, he grew up in New York, too, they grooved. Just as he knew they would.

She'd lived downtown, in TriBeCa, she told him, had gone to the Little Red Schoolhouse on Bleecker Street, and had grown up an independent, strong little kid raised by an extremely cool single mom.

While Joss stopped short of telling her he'd grown
up on the Upper East Side, attended pricey private
schools, and grown up a sheltered little rich kid,
with a Donald Trump–like, only-worse, father, there
was enough of a common vibe to keep them laughing, reminiscing, connecting. And for the first time
in eighteen months? Damn, he missed the city!

When they reached the car, he asked, "So, where
to now? Dancing? Movies? Sports bar? Minigolf?
Night court?"

"Don't quit your day job," she quipped. "You are
so not the last comic standing. You know where we
both want to go."

She wasn't suggesting—?

Harper crossed her arms, amused. "While slurping down oysters, have we not been ogling the most
amazing beach ever?"

Joss grinned. "That was my next idea." Dude,
it'd been his *only* idea, from the moment he'd found
a hapless Harper in the kitchen, distracted by her
woes, almost burning the place down. He wanted to
rescue her, wanted to take her here, cradle her on
the warm sands of the beach.

"So, there's a path down there," she said. "Obviously you've been here before. Which qualifies you
to lead us."

Girl was right. Joss knew where they would go,
how to get there, and what he needed to bring. He

flipped open the trunk of the car, retrieved his black Taylor acoustic. He'd taken this guitar down to the beach multiple times, and let the songs find him. Cheesy much? But who was he to question a creative rush, where it had begun—or why?

Harper arched her eyebrows when she saw the guitar. "A beach concert?"

Joss motioned for her to follow him. He led her down a wooded path that began at the back of the Beachcomber. It sloped downward, looped around, straightened out for a stretch, only to curve again. Without warning, Harper broke into a run, shooting down the dunes as fast she could. Joss didn't need an invite to join her, nor did he ask permission to grab her hand as they ran in step. The wind flew in their faces, Harper's hair fanned out, wild and free and untamed as the girl herself. The path became steep as it neared the beach, but no way would Harper slow the pace. They hit the sand hard, winded and laughing at their childish silliness.

At the shoreline, Harper panted and bent over, hands cupping her knees. "Dumb fun. Bummer you had to do it dragging your strings." She dug into her pocket for a scrunchie and tied her hair back.

Joss flung the guitar over his shoulder. He wondered if, by the moonlight, she could see the decals on his guitar strap. Backstage passes of the groups he'd toured with in the past year and a half. Would she recognize the one that belonged to Jimi Jones? And if she did, would she react?

Harper kicked her sandals off and declared, "I gotta feel the sand between the toes."

They meandered down the beach, following the shoreline as it curved westward, until they came to the cove that had been his destination all along. The dune scoop beneath an overhang formed by an outcropping of rock, a cozy shelter he'd discovered a few weeks ago that had become his songwriting haven.

Joss and Harper sat in silence until he corralled his courage and began to strum the lustrous guitar. He played "Better Things," an old chestnut written by the Kinks' Ray Davies that this cover band, Babylon Sad—the one Joss had toured with just before his Jimi Jones gig—used to sing every night. It wasn't a real mainstream song, but Joss had a hunch Harper knew the words.

She chimed in: "Here's wishing you the bluest sky . . ."

Joss smiled. Not only did she indeed know all the words, she had a strong, sure voice as well. He could compare it with a Chryssie Hynde, or . . . to a female version of Harper's father. But he didn't. Instead, they harmonized and ended with: "*I hope tomorrow you'll find better things. . . .*"

Joss told her, "When I was on tour with that cover band, dude, they sang this every night. I should be sick of it. Only I'm not. It still gets to me."

"Well, sure," Harper said. "It's unselfish. It's about what you want for someone else."

It didn't escape Joss that Harper took him for an unselfish kinda guy. He kinda liked it.

Harper continued. "Anyway, that's what good music is all about. It's more than happy-go-hooky lyrics and a count-to-four backbeat. There's truth in them there words. When they hook up with soul-stirring music—that's gonna haunt you."

Josh lit up. Bingo. He'd been right about her all along. Harper Jones had inherited way more than her famous father's quirky half-smile, wiry build, sarcastic wit, and bedroom eyes. Whether she even knew it or not, she had his musical genius. It lay deep in the DNA, no escape, though Joss suspected she'd been trying, probably her whole life.

Now. He might not get another moment like this. To tell her all, not just that he knew who she really was, but to come clean about himself. And knowing that, hope she could still be into him. He was just about to spill, when Harper interrupted.

"Do you know 'The Freshman'? By Verve Pipe?" she asked.

He did, but would rather have played "Your Body Is a Wonderland," by John Mayer. However, "The Freshman" it would be. *"For the life of me I cannot believe we'd ever die for these sins, we were merely freshmen."*

And so, they music-melded, Joss (née Joshua) Wanderman (née Sterling) and Harper Jones. An eavesdropper, someone crouched on the cliff above them, would have heard snippets of songs, attempts at harmony, convivial conversation that coiled and wound around itself like a helix, punctuated with lighthearted laughter and groans of "Eww . . . cheesy!"

And Joss never got to say what he knew he ought to.

But dude, it wasn't just vocal cords and guitar chords at play here. His heart—if that didn't deserve an "eww . . . cheesy!"— *that's* what was singing.

Joss didn't dare play a Jimi Jones song. Instead, he went into a riff Harper couldn't possibly know.

Only she did. "That's an original. You wrote it, didn't you?"

"What do you think?" He looked up hopefully.

"I think"—she paused and drew a treble clef in the sand—"it's amazing. Not that it doesn't need work!"

Joss crossed his arms over his guitar. Right—let her just try to keep lying to him.

She gave it up, palms raised in an "I surrender" gesture. "So what, yeah, I'm somewhat musical. I have a feel for it. At least I know what's good when I hear it, and what sucks."

"You know more than that. You also know how to fix what's not working."

"Maybe," she conceded. "It needs a full D with a seventh for accent. There, after the A minor. Build the chorus and finish with the power chord. Right now, you got it all in minors."

Whoa. She'd been schooled, and he was more impressed than he thought he'd be.

Harper continued, "Anyway, what are the lyrics?"

She'd opened the door, and Joss blasted through. "There aren't any. I'm neither lyricist nor poet. But I know someone who is. Fortuitously, she's right here."

Harper chuckled. "And so, ladies and gentlemen, we come to 'the agenda' portion of the program."

Joss feigned bewilderment, but couldn't keep up the ruse. He didn't want to. "Harper Jones, will you write something for this?"

She pressed her lips together, dug up a stone, and tossed it toward the ocean. "Maybe I already have."

Silence.

"But?"

More silence.

Joss put the guitar down. He got it. The poem she'd written, the one that would fit this song? She wasn't sharing. "Not ready to trust me with it," he speculated.

"Not so much," Harper conceded, now drawing

a wavy musical staff in the sand with her forefinger. "But don't take it personally. Trust is overrated."

"Like relationships?" he guessed.

"Dude"—Harper threw another stone toward the water—"relationships are like cotton candy: all pretty and sparkly and sugary and tempting. But the minute you take a bite, what happens? They dissolve and leave you with tooth decay. Relationships that involve trust are bad for you."

"You can't really believe that." Joss bristled.

"Can't I? What more proof do you need than the saga of the lovebird living in the share house with us? Tell me *that's* not fucked up."

Joss tensed. "You mean Mitch? He's still crazy about Leonora. So what do you know that no one else does?"

"You know it too. The difference is, you intuited it, and I saw it. I saw *her*."

Harper drew her knees into her chest. She spoke softly, recounting the scene she'd walked in on, Leonora and Grace Hannigan's father under the sheets. Joss's stomach sank lower with each word. He pounded the sand. "Oh, man! I knew somethin' wasn't cool the first time I met her. Shit, poor Mitch."

"Do we tell him?" Harper's voice was barely above a whisper. "We can't, right? I mean . . ."

Joss shook his head sadly. "No choice. We have

to. It sucks that he's the one to get his heart carved up. Leonora is his dream girl. She represents everything he's worked for. Everything she offers, it's the life he wants."

"The trick," Harper said, lifting her chin defiantly, "is not to want."

No! That's not it at all! That can't be it. Because right now, Joss wanted. Oh, how he wanted. Badly. Harper Jones was the most enchanting girl he'd ever seen. She was not just stirringly beautiful, but profound, and proud, and poetic, and . . . and . . . funny! God *damn*, she was funny.

She was also closed for business—she'd just said as much. Once upon a time she'd wanted—the boy's name was Luke—and look where it had gotten her. Once burned, forever scorched. This decision, irrefutable, made at age seventeen. Joss gazed into her astoundingly light blue-gray eyes. She was meltingly beautiful, this "sweet child o' mine," he thought lyrically. He loved the way the little tendrils of curls escaped her every effort to tie her hair back, how they brushed her temples, framed her cocoa face. Who could hurt a girl like this? Who could rip her heart apart, so she'd never give it away again? Joss couldn't understand.

Like the tide that can't stop nature's pull back out to sea, Joss could not help himself. He pulled her close, drew his arms around her, tipped her head up, and kissed her. He wanted to be gentle, tried to be, but God, she tasted sweet. And Joss had never been this hungry.

She didn't reject him. In spite of what she said, Harper parted her lips, and at first simply let him kiss her. When she tentatively began responding, her passion, her hunger did not match his. But it was enough. Enough to let him know he wasn't stranded here in head-over-heels land, alone with these feelings.

If she would ever acknowledge them, if they'd ever share another kiss like that, Joss could not predict. As soon as they pulled apart, they got up and retraced their footsteps back through the dunes, climbed uphill until they reached the restaurant and the car.

Joss slipped a Death Cab for Cutie CD in to cover the strained silence between them. It wasn't until they were turning onto Cranberry Lane that Joss found his voice. "Hey look, I didn't plan for that to happen, but I'm not sorry it did. It was just a very cool evening, and I got caught up in the moment, in you."

Harper wasn't even looking at him.

"It won't happen again, not if you don't want it to," he said, unconvincingly.

Still no response. He leaned over and tenderly

brushed her hair behind her ear. "Just don't hate me, okay?"

Harper pointed straight ahead, to the share house. "Something's wrong," was all she said.

## *Violated*

"I been violated!" Mandy shrieked, jerkily stomping around her room and clawing at her hair. Hysterical and hammered, she came off more comical than convincing. "The fuckers freakin' stripped me!"

Alefiya had come flying in. The scene mirrored the one in her own room. Drawers and closet doors yanked open, their contents rifled through and flung all over the floor—even the mattresses pulled off the beds, and turned over.

Ali took a deep calming breath, as much for herself as for the drama queen. "You weren't personally violated, Mandy. It's bad karma to exaggerate."

Mandy fired bloodshot daggers at her. "They pawed through my personal belongings! Like"—she hiccuped—"animals! They took my stuff!"

"Exactly," Ali reasoned. "Your *stuff*. Not you."

Mandy ramped up her rage. "You don't get it, do you? You . . . you . . . third-world freak! They raped my room. What would you call it?"

A robbery. Because that's exactly what it was.

What it *wasn't*, Alefiya deduced, as she tried calming the caterwauling girl, was random.

It was rare that all six of them were out at the same time. Whoever was responsible for this home invasion either knew that, or had been watching the house. She shivered.

By coincidence, Ali and Mandy had returned home roughly the same time, around 1:30 a.m. "Leaf," as Jeremy liked to call her, had been out with him, plus Sharif and Lisa. After weeks of trying, the trio finally succeeded in cheering Alefiya up. She still felt guilty about the way the party had ended, but as her friends kept reminding her, she was starting to accept that her intentions had been pure and, in the end, that no one got seriously hurt, or sick, or actually arrested.

"No harm, no foul"—an expression she'd learned over the summer—seemed to apply.

More importantly, Jeremy pointed out, it was over. Time to let it go, cheer up, enjoy the rest of the summer.

Still, Ali shied away from inviting them in that night. Her once carefree *mi casa es su casa* open-door policy didn't feel right anymore. So Jeremy settled for walking her halfway up the gravel drive and leaving her with a sweet, lingering kiss. She responded in kind, draping her arms around his shoulders and holding him close. Ali knew this: Summer's end would not mean the end of them. This boy was a keeper. That's when real problems would kick in. Ali shuddered, imagining her strict father going apoplectic at the sight of the very *not* Indian Jeremy LaSalle.

It was the taste of Jeremy's full lips on her own Ali was replaying when she turned the key in the front door. It didn't click. Hmmm. Harper was the only one who'd said she'd be home tonight—so why wasn't the door locked? Harper, being from New York City, was kind of paranoid about that.

Nervous, Alefiya gently pushed the door open a few inches. Clarence streaked through her legs, and in a flash, was down driveway and into the street.

Ali dropped her purse and bolted after him. She didn't see the car rounding the corner—only heard the sound of tires screeching to a sudden stop.

"Clarence!" she screamed. No! No . . . please . . . don't let him be hurt, she prayed, running into the street. Clarence was inches from the car, but thankfully, unharmed. Beyond grateful, she picked the errant ferret up, wondering how he'd gotten out of his cage.

Tim Johnson, Mandy's "live-in" boyfriend, was at the wheel. Mandy, in the passenger seat, leaned out the window. "Your pet rat wuz almos' roadkill. We gotta try harder next time, don' we, Timmy-cakes?"

Mandy was drunk. Well, at least she wasn't driving—that was something. Cradling Clarence, Ali turned away and strode back to the house. Behind her, the car door opened, Mandy toppled out, and Tim drove away. Before she could inquire why Tim wasn't staying, Mandy snarled, "Wus this crap on the front lawn? Who left the upstairs windows open? What'd you do, dump your discards out the window?"

Ali hadn't even noticed the lawn, still scraggly despite her efforts to spruce it up. What was her tapestry beach blanket doing out there? And her embroidered peasant blouse? Whose sandal was that?

"Pisshead!" Mandy drunkenly blasted. "What'd you do, throw my shoe out with your garbage? That's 'n expensive shoe, you numbnut!"

Ali was annoyed, borderline panicky now. The unlocked door, Clarence out of his cage, clothes hanging out the window and on the lawn. She grabbed Mandy by the elbow. "Sober up. We better see what's going on."

Mandy yanked away from her. "Are you kidding? I'm not goin' in there."

"Then stay outside and call the police. I'll go in."

Ali braced herself, afraid of what she might find. Something had happened—oh God, what if Harper was in there?

She wasn't.

Nor was anything else.

The living room was bare; the only clue that furniture had once been there, the indentations in the carpet from the coffee tables and lamps. Unless the stuff had been repossessed or something, they'd been robbed. Big time. Ali's hand flew to her mouth, her eyes went wide. She dashed into the kitchen—same story: table and chairs, coffeemaker, microwave, gone. Only the refrigerator remained, but like the cabinets, the door was open, its contents strewn all over the floor.

Mandy noisily trotted in, calling out brazenly. "Whoever you are, we got a rat! A poisonous big ol' rat—and we're not afraid to use him! He's got teeth! Come out with your hands up!"

Ali rolled her eyes. If Mandy wasn't so ludicrous, it'd be funny. "No one's here," she told her. "They took everything. Did you call the police?"

"They took our stuff?" Horrified, Mandy lurched toward the stairs, groping for the railing. She stumbled several times, anyway, on her way upstairs.

Mandy was on her hands and knees, wailing now as she attacked the hills of sartorial wreckage. "They took"—hiccup—"my good stuff. My lingerie! I saved up for all that stuff! Even my scrapbook." She turned her tear-stained face to Ali. "What'd they want with that? It's personal—it's my dreams. . . ." She trailed off, her nose running, and sobbed into her hands.

"It's just material possessions. They can be replaced." Ali searched for a tissue.

"No they can't!" Mandy shrieked, and ran to the bathroom.

Ali guessed Mandy, drunk and distraught, had not summoned the police, so she went downstairs to use the landline in the kitchen. She had one hand on the phone when she heard Katie come in squealing. "Oh my God! What happened in here?"

"We got robbed," Ali yelled to her.

"We got robbed?" Katie repeated dumbly. "Who'd want to rob this dump? There's like nothing worth taking."

Ali shook her head. Maybe to Katie, there wasn't—the roomie upstairs would beg to disagree. As Alefiya gave the address to the cops, she heard Katie make a decision.

"I better call Mitch."

Calling Mitch was Katie's default reaction to anything that required a responsible adult to take over. It was at that moment Ali realized Mandy had probably been right about Katie all along. She *was* underage. And more: had been sheltered, pampered, taken care of all her life. It begged the question, already asked by the others, what was Katie doing here?

Katie flipped her phone shut and reported, "Mitch'll be here in a second. He was just turning onto the block. He'll handle everything."

Ali squeezed Katie's shoulders lightly. "The damage has been done, and thank god, no one got hurt. The police are on the way. There's really nothing for Mitch to handle."

*That* turned out to be a really good thing. For this time? Mitch was incapable of handling anything. For the first time, in the face of crisis, their can-do den dad suddenly could *not*. Their lean-on-me hero became unhinged. Neither calm, nor cool, and far from collected, Mitch raced through the living room, directly into his bedroom, and very noisily freaked out. "My money! They stole the ring money. Every cent I've made this summer is gone!"

Ali and Katie, who'd followed, stood in Mitch's doorway, paralyzed. Just like in the other bedrooms, it looked like a tornado had touched down: The mattress had been turned over, sheets stripped off, pillowcases gone—used to haul away anything that could be stuffed into them.

Steadfast Mitch was in full-frontal meltdown, pounding the walls, screaming like a Mandy-banshee. "The bastards! The rotten, fucking bastards! I'll kill them!" He kicked the bed. "How'd they fucking know? How'd they get in? Through the fucking window?" He railed at the window, drew his arm back, and before anyone could stop him, smashed his fist through the glass.

"No! Stop it! Stop!" Summoning her prodigious strength, Ali pulled Mitch away from the window. Katie rushed to the bathroom to grab a towel to wrap around his bloodied wrist.

Mandy came thumping down the stairs. The glass-shattering commotion must have pulled her out of her personal pity-party. One look at Mitch, she sobered up. Pushing Katie aside, she barked, "Give me the towel. Let me do that."

Ali was almost impressed.

"Mitch! Get a hold of yourself!" Mandy commanded. Then her voice softened to a nurturing cajole. "Come on, honey, let's see if I learned anything from all those first aid lessons we got at the Dorchester Boys and Girls Club."

Ali registered surprise. So did Katie—for a microsecond. Then, the petite powerhouse leaped into action. "I'm getting duct tape, or whatever Mitch said he bought. All that stuff's in the bathroom, right?"

Eventually, Mitch succumbed to Mandy's ministrations, though it took all three girls to hold him down and stem the bleeding. If only, Ali mused miserably, they could have a similar effect on his psyche.

Stalwart, unflappable Mitchell James Considine was falling apart before their eyes.

"You don't understand," Mitch whimpered. "How am I going to propose? How am I going to get her to marry me? My life is ruined!"

Worse than devastated, Mitch looked defeated. He sat on the edge of the bed, head in his hands, sobbing inconsolably. There was nothing Alefiya and Mandy could do but sit on either side of him, stroke his back, and try in vain to console him.

Katie asked what no one else dared. "Why was all that cash in the house? Why didn't you put it in a bank?"

Bad move. Mitch freaked all over again. "Because, Missy McMoney-bags, I got a better deal from a jeweler who only takes cash. Not something *you* would understand! And besides, I didn't think we had anything to worry about living here—why would robbers pick this shithouse to target?!"

Mandy, Ali, and a stunned, red-faced Katie teamed up to soothe Mitch, tried to get him to settle down, until the cops arrived and they could take him to the hospital.

Such was the scene when a stunned Joss and Harper blasted in to find them a few minutes later. The sight of Mitch so pathetic stopped them cold.

Ali wiped away tears as she filled them in. "I called the police. They're on the way. I don't know what else to do."

Mandy began to bark out orders. "Finally! You managed to show up. Now make yourself useful and take Mitch to the emergency room. His hand's gonna need stitches."

With lightning speed, Joss took hold of Mitch, ignoring his distraught housemate's cries to "Let me go, you asshole! I have to get my money back!"

"Now you, Princess!" Mandy turned to Katie. "Your type always has some prescription drugs around—go get something for Mitch."

Katie looked scandalized. Ali was about to intervene, when Mandy shrieked, "Just do it!"

Katie returned with two orange pills in her palm. "Xanax," she told Joss. "That should do the trick."

"Good," Mandy said condescendingly. "Princess isn't such a pea-brain after all." She turned to Joss. "Force him to take them. He needs sedating."

The cops arrived just after Joss left for the emergency room with a still-protesting Mitch. The Hyannis Police had sent two detectives, who went through the share house with the four girls, helping them catalog what had been stolen.

It was a long list. The thieves had been equal opportunity: They'd hauled off anything of even remote value. Aside from all their furniture, among the missing was Mitch's money, his laptop, Mandy's "designer accessories," trinkets, and, strangely, her scrapbook; Ali's embroidered silk sari—she had no idea what she'd tell her parents about its loss—and Harper's last paycheck. Joss, at the emergency room with Mitch, would fill in his missing items later; though Mandy was positive he owned several guitars, not a one remained in his room now.

The detectives repeated Ali's words of wisdom: "Just be glad no one was hurt.

"Besides," they added, "*could* be the owners of the house even have insurance. You could get the furniture replaced right away." They took everyone's statements, and copious notes. By the time they were ready to leave, they confirmed Ali's worst fear when she'd first discovered the robbery.

"No sign of forced entry," determined the young-looking detective, who'd introduced himself as MacMillan. "If you're absolutely sure the last person out locked up, then we're left with two scenarios." He paused, and let his partner spell it out.

"The thief was one of you, or it's someone with access to your keys," said Detective Ronson with a shrug. "So you gotta be asking yourselves, is anyone's key missing? Did one of you duplicate a key and give it to someone? What about the two guys you live with? One of them a little shady?"

Ali, Harper, Katie—even Mandy—said absolutely nothing.

Naturally, the detectives promised to do everything they could to find the perps and recover the stolen belongings. Before leaving, MacMillan wagged his finger at them. "Know what I think? One of you knows more than you're saying. This was an inside job."

Ali felt herself crumbling. It didn't take a sage or seer to know exactly how this was going to play out.

**19**

Cape Cod

# The Blame Game

Mitch could not look at Alefiya without glaring. He didn't bother to hide his disgust with her. Or with himself.

Saturday afternoon, he jogged along the shoreline, his bandaged right hand still throbbing nearly a week later. Damn! Why hadn't he trusted his instinct instead of convincing himself that Ali's slovenliness was just a minor nuisance? Her laissez-faire attitude was a major character flaw; he should have nipped it in the bud before it led to disaster.

Mandy had nailed it, right from the jump. But Mitch had convinced himself he wasn't judgmental like that anymore. Just because they'd grown up in poverty and the small-minded attitudes of the city housing projects didn't mean *he* still was like that.

He'd gotten out. He'd earned a scholarship to Harvard, he'd evolved, he didn't make snap judgments about people based on one character trait. He was worldly, worthy of Leonora and her family, primed and poised to jump into that life, as if he'd been born to it.

And now that was gone. Slipped through his grasp like sand through his fingers. All because the money he'd put in the "Engagement Ring" envelope, all that he'd saved by living in a cheapo place, by playing janitor so he could pay less in rent, everything he'd so carefully put aside to buy his better life—all of it was gone, stolen.

All because Ali had been sloppy. He was convinced of it. How many keys had she lost? Like he didn't know Harper had replaced them. Katie had snitched.

How many keys had Ali—despite her denials—given to her "friends"? She used the place as a damn crash pad, which *he'd* tried to curtail. But Joss, the big strong silent hero, had defended her, insisted she had the right to as many guests as she wanted. Mitch wondered how Joss, who'd lost two precious guitars in the robbery, felt about Ali now?

Mitch cursed himself for not dealing with her right after the party. That's when he ought to have shut her down, kicked her out for breaking the rules.

She'd have gone, too, ridden her guilt on the next bus back to Tufts.

But no, he hadn't handled it that way. He was bigger than that. Any fool knew there'd be a party; he just didn't know who'd break the rule first. When it turned out to be Alefiya Sunjabi, he was secretly glad. By taking it all in stride, he'd shown that he bore her no prejudice, treated her as he'd have treated Katie had she invited a hundred strangers to trash their house.

Good call, he chastised himself bitterly as he finally ran out of steam, panting for breath. Schmuck.

Without the money, he couldn't hope to buy a ring. Without use of his right hand, he couldn't even work for the next couple of weeks. Let alone take on a second job, which he contemplated. So much for building the ring fund back up. Without it, what did he have to offer the ever-more-distant Leonora?

Katie knew this was Ali's fault. Unlike Mitch, she couldn't show her contempt since, comparatively, she'd barely lost anything in the robbery. Just her Vera Bradley suitcases, which the thieves probably used to carry out their booty. Which sucked, since she'd planned to sell them. But it was a far cry from having your money, your guitars, or, like Mandy, your jewelry (tacky as it was) stolen.

The cash Katie had been saving was every bit as crucial to her life as Mitch's was to his. (So were the prescription drugs she'd been hoarding, which she could totally sell.)

But she'd been cagier than transparent, trusting Mitch. She hadn't left her currency in an envelope underneath her mattress! Hello? Her Charlesworth brain was always working: Even her oblivious mother knew that much about her.

True, the low-class losers who'd ripped and slashed their way through the cottage had come close, ransacking the closet she and Harper shared. But even they wouldn't bother with a pile of extra rolls of toilet paper—let alone, think to look inside the hollow cardboard tubes of the Charmin. All four triple-ply were stuffed with bundles of cash, every bit of what she'd earned and/or snagged from Brian had been squirreled away. She'd outfoxed the robbers.

Katie sat on the floor, legs pretzeled beneath her, and counted her cash. She was up to $3,000. She felt relieved, if not safe. She'd ducked the cops the night of the party, but the investigation of the robbery—they'd taken the names of everyone in the house—meant there now existed a police record of exactly where she was. Anyone could find her now, anyone could find the truth. The diva was in a dive, partying on someone else's dime every night, while she toiled in some drone job during the day. Not for charity or social causes, but because she needed the money.

Her parents could find her, if they wanted to. Anyone could.

Here it was, August, and she still had no real plan to escape the spiderweb, the mesh of lies her stupid parents had woven, to elude being punished along with them, for nothing she had done.

So maybe Nate? She didn't know exactly how he could help, but he was smart, as well as rich. Maybe if he understood her predicament, he'd think of a way out.

As for Alefiya Sunjabi? If Katie never saw her again, it would be too soon.


Harper stuck up for Ali. "You have no proof," she scolded Katie.

"It's circumstantial," she told Mitch.

Those two made no secret of their guilty verdict. Privately, though, as she sat on the beach writing in her journal, Harper conceded there was more than a good chance Ali's sloppy habits, and open-door policy, had indeed led to the robbery. She'd personally replaced Ali's lost keys twice.

Ali's denials counted for something, Harper reminded herself. She'd taken full responsibility for the party, had even ponied up as much of the damage-repair expenses as she could afford. If this rob-

bery had been her fault, Harper believed Alefiya
would own it.

But just because she hadn't intentionally
handed her keys to one of her guests didn't mean it
hadn't gone down that way. Who, aside from Alefiya, had so many random guests, anyway?

Harper gazed out at the ocean. A lone jogger
stopped to catch his breath.

Mitch.

She'd lived with him nearly two months now,
and stood by her first impression: J.Crew-guy was
stand-up, square-shouldered, straight-laced, and . . .
pure. Her heart broke, he was so misguided in his
misery.

What she wouldn't do to run up to him now,
take him by the shoulders, and shake some sense
into him. "Dude, you should thank Ali. Good you
can't buy the cheating bitch a ring. Leonora's not
worthy of you!"

Harper sat still. No way could she crush him
now—even Joss agreed. Now was not the time to tell
what Harper had seen.

Thinking about Joss, she went back to the poem
that'd go with Joss's music. She was into him, no
matter that she didn't want to be. She almost wished
he'd do something crappy, reveal his inner asshole.

Only, not. Joss had remained amazingly cool. He'd
lost two of his precious guitars, which he so didn't have

the money to replace—and yet, had not rushed to judgment, had sided with her in defending Ali.

"Hey, Shakespeare, ever thought-a writing a movie? That's where the money is."

Harper looked up and frowned. Mandy, in a barely there bikini, slinging a towel over her shoulder, plopped down in the sand next to her.

Crude, rude Mandy had been strangely subdued after the robbery, neither blaming nor supporting Ali. It had come out that she and Mitch were childhood friends—which now made a lot of sense to Harper. It explained tons about why these two opposites were so alike. And explained why Mitch's meltdown had pulled Mandy out of terminal self-absorption.

"How come you're not at Muscle Beach?" Harper inquired. "Isn't that where the daily manhunt takes place?"

Mandy slipped off her bikini top, exposing herself to the sun. "I need to get an all-over tan. My photo shoot is in a few days."

"You're not posing nude, are you?"

"Why? Ya worried about me?"

Harper found that she was. "I just wouldn't want to see you—or anyone— being exploited, or taken advantage of. That's all."

Harper was partly right about Joss. Losing his guitars *had* bummed him out, but not nearly as much as Mitch's behavior did. Joss had witnessed more than his share of meltdowns in twenty-one years, but he felt worst about this poor dumb housemate. All that pent-up good-guy rage had just spontaneously combusted! Mitch had not recovered emotionally—and he didn't even know the truth about Leonora yet.

It was Joss who went ahead and contacted the owners of the house. It hadn't surprised him that they didn't, in fact, have theft insurance. Nor did they care to replace the furniture. The summer share clients would just have to deal. Soon enough, it was all good riddance, anyway. They should count themselves lucky the owners of the shit-shack weren't suing them!

Joss had hung up on the sleaze bags, knowing they'd be living in a bare house. The likelihood of the police recovering the stolen items was slim. Of course, he could easily replace everything—including Mitch's money. It'd mean nothing to him, really, his trust funds, all the other accounts in his name? They'd barely register the withdrawal. It would mean, of course, alerting his father to his whereabouts and risking being pulled back home.

Joss would've done it, anyway—running from that life seemed less important to him now—but if he did, he'd have to expose himself to the group. To Harper. She'd find out he'd been lying about who he was. Worse, if he replaced everything that'd been stolen, Mitch would go buy Leonora's ring. He couldn't let that happen.

Mandy was fuming. But not at Ali. She wasn't sure whether Miss Piggy had done anything or not. She simply couldn't be bothered sticking up for her. She had a photo shoot to get ready for.

Why had the thieves stolen her lingerie? What kind of sick pervs would do that? That was the big puzzle, she thought, as the sun's afternoon rays caressed her topless body. Of course they hadn't taken Alefiya's ugly, oversize garb, or Harper's ratty hippie chick rags—but why not Katie's exorbitantly expensive designer duds? Why *her* cherished collection of teddies, and thongs, and push-up bras? Why her accessories? Her jewelry had been costume, cheap stuff, but it was all she had.

Once she got famous, she thought, closing her eyes, she could afford the real things: those chandelier earrings, bejeweled belts, Judith Lieber beaded clutches, even real Manolos. Mandy licked her lips, picturing herself decked out royally. Like the outfit Paris Hilton wore, the one she'd cut out and put in her scrapbook.

Unexpectedly, a tear slid out. Why the scrapbook? It was a piece of her soul, the one thing that truly was irreplaceable. But, she rationalized, using a corner of her towel to dry her eye, the scrapbook chronicled her dreams. Once they became reality, she'd have tossed it out herself. So maybe the thief had done her a favor. Saved her the trouble.

What she didn't need was the distraction of Mitch. But she could not help herself. Mandy was worried about him. The dumb fuck was talking about taking on a second job! Like he wasn't wearing himself down as it was, doing that hoity-toity bitch Leonora's business. He told her he was thinking of applying for a weekend lifeguard gig at Craigville Beach, soon as his hand healed.

"That, *plus* the tennis thing?" She'd been disbelieving. "What're ya, nuts? No one's worth killing yourself over, Mitch."

He brushed her aside. "You go to that beach all the time. All I'm gonna have to do is sit up in the chair and relax. No one goes in the water. Everyone's too busy hooking up."

Mandy wanted to believe that. But she didn't.

"Into each life, a little rain must fall." That was one of the meant-to-be uplifting clichés Ali's mom said to cheer her up. "The purpose of bad things happening," she'd remind her daughter, "is to make you appreciate the good things even more." When Ali was a child, she'd believed that. She was no longer a child.

It took a lot to unhinge Ali, make her question her beliefs, but the climate at 345 Cranberry Lane, the "scorn-fest," as Harper had called it, was making her come awfully close. The amount of animosity aimed at her weighed her down. It threatened to crush her spirit. She had misplaced a key here or there, that much was true. But she hadn't *given* anyone a key.

And okay, she hadn't done a background check on the few people—not that many!—who'd slept over. But Alefiya trusted herself: She was perceptive about people. Those she befriended, those she'd been generous to, were not thieves.

No way was the robbery her fault.

Not one of her housemates believed her. Some were open-faced hostile; others said things behind her back. Didn't matter. She knew they all blamed her. The words "We want you to leave" had not been said aloud, but it was all over Mitch's face. Of all the share house people, his contempt was the one she could bear least. When a week had gone by and the anger toward her had not abated, she seriously did consider packing up and going home early.

Jeremy talked her out of it. "What if we search and dig up the missing keys?" he'd suggested. "If they're in the house, which I bet they are, maybe the others will at least *consider* it wasn't your fault."

Ali didn't think that would help.

The next day, Jeremy had done the oddest thing. He'd arrived at the share house with a lantern. Ali was bewildered. "If you've come to help me search for the keys, a flashlight might work better."

Jeremy set the lantern down on her dresser and recited: "'From falsehood lead me to truth, from darkness lead me to light. . . .'"

Ali's hand flew to her mouth. A direct quote from Hindu scripture, usually recited on the festival of Diwali, on which people lit rows of lamps along walkways and gardens.

Jeremy blushed. "It's a little early for your holiday, but I thought maybe you needed this now."

The glow, from deep within Alefiya's soul, was brighter than a block of lanterns.

# *Happy Birthday, Katie!*

"Surprise!" Two voices, a guy's and a girl's, rang out, accompanied by the sudden opening and shutting of the screen door.

Katie froze. Sunday afternoon, she, Harper, and Ali had joined forces to clean the kitchen, since Mandy was primping for her shoot, Mitch was at his weekend lifeguard gig, and Joss was still asleep. An uneasy truce had been reached since the robbery three weeks ago. Ali had found the missing keys. It had not convinced anyone of her innocence.

"Sur-PRISE!" The tandem voices again, coming from the living room now.

Katie, in scraggly cut-offs and a baseball cap, had been sponging off the stove. Harper, in overalls, was cleaning the refrigerator shelves, and Ali, in a long boy's T-shirt, had just started sweeping the floor.

"Anybody home?" the female visitor called out as two sets of footsteps came closer.

Katie knew the voice all too well. Her heart lurched. It was at that moment she truly realized how much she'd missed Lily McCoy, who had materialized, out of the blue, willowy, tan, toned, absolutely beaming—right in the kitchen archway.

Lily had arrived neither alone, nor empty-handed. A tall, angular hottie, blond hair brushing his forehead, was at her side, holding a huge Ziploc bag of live lobsters in one hand, a bottle of Cristal champagne in the other.

Lily herself was decked out in a Marc Jacobs mini, matching tank top with designer shrug. She carried a Dooney & Bourke clutch as her armpit accessory, and swung a plaid Burberry shopping bag in front of her. "Happy Birthday, Katie!" she sang out, running to embrace her. "I missed you so much!"

Katie stood rigidly, allowing Lily to hug her (while the swinging shopping bag grazed her butt). She let the soaking wet rag in her hand drop to the floor (instead of staining Lily's half-cardigan top, like she should have done).

Lily backed off and tilted her head sympathetically. "I know I'm not your favorite person right now, but best friends do *not* let birthdays go uncelebrated."

Katie murmured, "Best friends don't abandon each other for—"

"This is Luke," Lily said brightly, her arm snaking around the cruelly thin (for a guy) waist of her boyfriend, the guy she'd deemed her "better offer." Lily started to say something about "It's time you two met" when, jarringly, a pair of earsplitting noises rocked the house.

The refrigerator slammed shut and with such fury, the bottles in the door crashed into one another. At the same moment, the Cristal champagne smashed to the floor along with the bag of lobsters. Everyone jumped.

That's when Katie realized, to her horror, that Harper was right there.

And when Luke learned, to his horror, that Harper was right there.

The exes stared at each other, Harper's eyes full of fury, Luke's wide with the fear of the guilt-ridden.

Ali stared at the floor. The lobsters had crawled out of the bag.

Lily stammered, "What's going on? I don't get it."

"You wouldn't," Katie practically spat. "It involves human emotions."

"Harper?" Luke advanced toward her. "What are you doing here?"

Harper pressed her back against the fridge and raised her palms defensively.

Ali, now clutching a lobster in each hand, inserted herself between Luke and a quivering Harper. "I don't know who you are," she said, not unkindly, "but I get the sense that Harper doesn't want you coming too close. Maybe you and your friend should visit with Katie in another room."

"Harper, I'm so totally sorry—" Katie began, but Ali shooed them out. "Give her a chance to get herself together," Ali whispered. "I'll clean this mess up—call me if you need support."

"Thank you," Katie managed to whisper.

"What happened to all the furniture?" Lily asked, surveying the bare living room. "Is it out being cleaned or something?"

"It's just out," Katie answered.

Settling herself on the only place to perch, the low fireplace mantel, Lily crossed her long legs and patted the cold stone for Luke to sit next to her.

Like a well-trained puppy, he obeyed.

"Well," Lily exhaled dramatically, "that didn't go exactly as I'd hoped."

"Lily, what are you doing here?" Katie hissed, standing over her. "And how could you bring . . . him? Well, I guess neither of you knew. . . ." Katie sighed. Luke squirmed guiltily.

Lily widened her eyes, affecting a wounded look. "I want to make up, Katie. You haven't answered a single one of my calls, my e-mails, IMs—nada. You act like I don't even exist."

You should have thought of that two and a half months ago, Katie thought bitterly, her hands on her hips.

"It wasn't exactly easy to find you," Lily complained, "just so you know. I went through a lot."

Not easy? Katie thought. It *would* have been impossible if not for the robbery and, probably, the big mouth of Taylor Ambrose.

Lily whined, "Who is that girl, anyway, in the kitchen? What's her saga?"

"Harper." They said it together—Katie angrily, Luke still in shock, softly.

"Her name is Harper Jones," Katie said, "and in case you didn't get the subtext of the little drama, she and your boyfriend used to be involved. Very involved. Very recently."

Luke coughed self-consciously, unsure if he should confirm, deny, or bail.

"Fine." Lily brushed her lustrous hair back. "Now I know her name. But I don't know why your thong is in a knot. I'm not some villain."

Katie stared at Luke. It wasn't hard to see what Harper had fallen for. Luke Clearwater was obviously of mixed heritage. As in Harper's case, it worked. Luke's full lips, high, wide Johnny Depp cheekbones, and slight build hinted at an American

Indian father (as did his last name). His height, swimming-pool-blue eyes, silky blond hair screamed Scandinavian. The total effect *was* admittedly doable—if you were into the whole soft-spoken sensitivity vibe.

So what was Lily was doing with him? Lily was all about status conquests, jocks who rock, studs with style, popularity princes, and, lately, older guys just to piss off her parents.

What Luke saw in Lily? Duh. Katie herself had shouted the reason to a house full of partygoers:

Lily put out.

"I like sex, so what?" she used to justify her behavior to Katie, who had cautioned selectivity. Lily had called her bluff: "Pul-eeze. Sex is currency with you. You'll give it up, but only when you can get something you want badly enough in return. I'm not calculating like that."

Katie suddenly felt stupid standing over the treacherous twosome. She settled on the floor against the wall and folded her arms. She spoke to Luke. "You never told Lily about Harper?"

Lily spoke for him. "Luke might've mentioned it. Did you, sweetie?" Lily ran her finger along his thigh. "If he said her name, it totally didn't register. It's not like she's someone I even knew."

Katie's stomach twisted. Once, she would have said the same exact thing.

"Anyway, how were we supposed to know she was here? It's not like you gave me a clue," Lily challenged.

She had a point, Katie supposed. Still, the damage was done. Katie couldn't imagine what Harper was feeling right now. But her heart went out to her roommate.

"So would you like us to leave?" Lily posed the obvious question.

The sad truth was that Katie did not. She'd missed Lily desperately, their friendship, their "best of breed" lifestyle. That's what she was fighting to hold on to! That's what this summer was all about. If not for the Luke/Harper complication, she might have welcomed the olive branch visit, after a few grumbling minutes forgiven Lily, even asked for her (belated) help. Katie's capacity for holding a grudge just wasn't that large. Not unless there was something to be gained by withholding.

Lily saw Katie caving. "So how ya like being seventeen so far?"

Katie grimaced. "I barely noticed the date." Which was a lie. Being alone (and still poor!) on her birthday made her sad, so she'd chosen not to think about it. If Plan A had panned out, she would've bagged a kickass boyfriend with cash and cache by now, would've worked out a way to recoup her old life, secure her future. There would have been a reason to celebrate.

Lily nudged the shopping bag at her feet toward Katie. "Don't you want to see what I got you?"

Before Katie could answer, Luke rose. "I'll go hang in the car. Probably better if you two talk without me."

Lily sprang to her feet and wrapped her arms around his neck. "You don't mind, baby? You are sooo sensitive!" She kissed him openmouthed, way more suggestively than the scenario deserved. It was a very Lily moment.

"You want to know what I'm doing with him," Lily declared, like that was the most important of the million things on Katie's list.

"He's hardly your type," she acknowledged.

Lily smiled wickedly. "Oh, but he *is*. I'm in a new phase, and he's just so young and delicious. So . . . mmmm . . . innocent. So *summer*. Y'know?"

Katie did, nauseatingly. Lily had lured this boy, was toying with him, playing the bad girl to his adoring naïf/virgin. She was test-driving a new power role, nothing more.

"I'm teaching him everything he needs to know," she confirmed with a wink. "It's so fulfilling. And—bonus: He writes me love poems."

"You're going to dump him after the summer," Katie stated.

Lily shrugged. "He goes to Boston Latin. Public

school. What do you think? And don't go all righteous on me. Denial does not become you—you'd do the same exact thing."

Katie reddened. "I have something more serious on my mind just now. Hello? Do you even remember why I'm here?"

"Of course I do."

"Then how could you just leave me stranded like that? And then, show up suddenly, expecting me to forget all about it?"

Lily shrugged, and pulled a cigarette from her bag. "Don't put me on the defense, Katie. You know it doesn't work with me. Luke showed up at my door one day, delivering pizza. And what can I say? You saw him. It was lust at first sight. And the . . . ahem . . . heart"—Lily patted her heart, but cast her eyes in a more southerly direction—"wants what it wants."

"That's your reason for abandoning me? You wanted to get laid?"

Now it was Lily's turn to pump up the volume. "How long have we been friends, Katie? And when, during the entire duration of our friendship, have we not put guys ahead of our plans? It's unspoken, but it rules: A hookup with a guy trumps plans you had with a girlfriend. I thought you'd understand."

"I didn't just hear that, Lily, because if I did, I don't even know you. This is not the same as canceling a trip to the mall for a hookup. There's a little more at stake here."

Lily leaned in toward her. "Don't push this, Katie."

"Don't *push* it? Consider yourself shoved. How could you turn your back on me like that?"

Dramatically, Lily lit her cigarette and inhaled. On the exhale, she said, "Maybe I gave your whole situation some thought. And maybe I realized that this summer, this whole getting-out-of-Boston thing was all about you. All about The Kick. And not for nothing, Katie? Maybe I got tired of being 'The Side Kick.'"

Katie gasped. She'd never known Lily was jealous of her. And that envy had led her to screw Katie the very first time she really, really needed a friend.

Katie sprang to her feet and yanked the cigarette from Lily's grasp just as the girl was exhaling, causing a coughing fit. She threw it into the fireplace.

Lily recovered quickly. "Look, I know you think your life is about to be over, your dad's business dealings and all that. But hello? You're Katie Charlesworth. I knew you'd figure something out. With or without me, you'd deal. So it's not like I was worried about you."

Katie thought her head would explode. She'd wanted to know how Lily had found her—had someone blabbed?—but at that moment, she was too enraged to care.

"Anyway, I really thought you'd have forgiven me by now," Lily said softly.

Katie barely heard her; she was screaming now. "How could you have the gall to think I would forgive you? You walked out on me the first time something serious in my life happened. After promising you would help. You swore! And you changed your mind, left me flat, because all this time you've been jealous of me? Impeccable timing, bitch!"

Oh shit, Katie was crying. Bawling.

# *Harper Hears Some Tuff Truths*

Harper's brain curled up into a fetal position. It would not allow her to process what she'd just seen. Unfortunately, she couldn't erase it either.

Luke—her Luke.

With Lily—Katie's bff Lily (*that* figured).

Luke and Lily, together as a couple, at the share house. Her hideaway.

After slamming the refrigerator, she'd fled, raced out the back door, down the beach to the water's edge.

Back in Boston, the awful day Luke had told her he'd found somebody else, Harper believed that if she saw him and his new "soul mate" holding hands and swapping saliva, the sight would send a knife to the heart. A pain so deep, death would be welcome. So she'd left Boston, avoided any possibility of running into them. Apparently, escape wasn't in the cards.

But a funny thing happened on the way to death-by-heartbreak, or maybe it just happened on her sprint from the house to the beach: She didn't die. She didn't even feel like dying. She'd seen her ex, she'd taken in Lily's skinny arm coil around his waist, and yeah, it reminded her of the way she and Luke used to walk with their hands slipped into each other's back pockets. That sight alone should have *flattened* her. But here she was, still standing. Digging her toe into the muddy sand, kicking it into the water.

She could breathe just fine. She could breathe *fire*.

Harper turned her back to the water and stalked toward the house. She needed a word with Luke, a little face time. She needed to barge right in on their reconciliation scene, Katie's and Lily's—and yank the boy away. "You don't mind if I borrow him?" she'd ask, not intending to wait for an answer.

Somehow, some way, Luke was going to give it up, explain to her what went wrong, why exactly he'd dumped her. What had she done to make him leave without warning, to render undone everything they had together?

And for Lily? How had this spoiled superficial bitch become his soul mate, his muse, forcing him to discard Harper like some crumpled-up verse that'll never be a poem, that isn't working?

It almost didn't matter what he said, she reflected, stomping onto the backyard deck. Just getting him to admit he'd shafted her was enough— and that the reason could *no way* have been sex. That would be just so trite, such a cliché! The Luke she knew and adored was just deeper than that; their relationship had meant so much, hadn't needed sex to prove it.

Harper had her hand on the back doorknob when she stopped suddenly. There was music playing. Norah Jones's jazzy romantic song: "Come Away with Me." The song had been this huge hit, could've been coming from any radio, anywhere. But Harper knew exactly where it was coming from. This was the live version, from the CD she'd bought for Luke.

She walked around the side of the house, to where Lily had parked her gas-guzzling status-symbol Esplanade SUV. Luke was in the driver's seat, his head bent forward, fiddling with the CD player. Had he meant for Harper to hear it? Was he summoning her?

No, this was *her* deal now. She flung open the passenger door and climbed in the car. She was confronting him—not the other way around.

"Harper!" His voice caught in his throat. Good, he hadn't seen her coming. The next thing he'd do was run his fingers through his silky hair; it's what he always did when he was nervous. That much hadn't changed.

But she had. Once, Luke's lopsided smile would've sent her reeling. Now, it just looked dumb. He mumbled, "I had no idea you were here. That was so not cool. I'm really sorry."

Not, "How are you?" Not, "I was such a shit." Not, "I've made a huge mistake, and now that I see you, I realize it." What had she expected? Harper was in shapeless, oversize cut-offs and a ratty T-shirt; Lily, decked in a sexy designer mini that left little unexposed. When she'd been with Luke, it had been a total mind-meld, the solace of true understanding of each other, combined with the rush of creating something together.

Lily offered him . . . ? Obvious, much?

What she'd needed to know only a few minutes ago—What are you doing with her? How could you leave me for her? What does she have that I don't? What did she use that I didn't?—was painfully clear. As transparent as Luke's trite little heart. Sex. All along it had been sex.

Harper's eyes flitted to the dashboard, to a piece of folded-up paper. It was familiar looking, the orange crinkly border distinctive. Funny Lily would have the same kind of paper as her old journal. Harper's heart seized as understanding dawned. Before Luke could stop her, she grabbed it.

*Some people come into your life,*
*and are gone forever.*
*Some people come into your life*
*and stay forever.*
*Some people come into your life*
*and leave footprints on your heart,*
*and you are forever changed.*

He'd used . . . Wite-Out? At the top, where she'd written "Dear Luke," he'd substituted "Dear Lily." And where she'd signed it, he'd deleted her name and signed his own.

"Wait!" Luke frantically tried to wrest the poem from her. "That's not—"

Harper didn't know whether to laugh or cry.

And then she knew everything she needed to know: Luke Clearwater wasn't worth wasting any emotion on whatsoever.

# Mandy's Big Break

She was shivering. It wasn't just the goose bumps raised on her bare arms and uncovered shoulders, or her fight to keep her teeth from chattering; Mandy Starr's chills ran to the bone. Something was not kosher in downtown Denmark, or whatever that expression was.

"Perfect! Oh, per-*fec*-tion, you are de-*lec*-table!" Joe Lester, the photographer Tim had introduced her to, was practically salivating as he ogled her through his camera lens. The emotion—if you could call it that—was seconded by Joe's "assistant," Skeever, who leered on approvingly. "Ain't she sweet," drooled the balding lump of lard, staring at her from the corner of the room. "Ain't she a treat."

Mandy stifled the urge to march up and drop him.

What was this mound of shit doing, anyway? Weren't assistants supposed to adjust the lighting, futz with those umbrella-things? Or at the very least, brandish a hairbrush, offer her a bottle of mineral water, or hello, lip gloss, anyone? Weren't they supposed to be assisting? The schlub leaning against the wall, hairy belly protruding from his too-short T-shirt, was a just a pig.

"Hey, Joe," she called to the photographer, "I'm freezing. Can we take a break so I can put a sweater on? Change outfits? I brought a real cute shrug."

"Not now," he responded, his eyes never leaving the digital camera. "Can't interrupt the creative process. Now, lower the strap on your other shoulder."

For the first set of photos, she'd chosen to pose in one of her favorite dresses, a designer copy of a lime green silk and satin sheath. The color brought out her eyes, the style—fitted bodice with a layered ruffle skirt—hinted at her curves. The shoulder straps were dotted with faux crystals, and Mandy liked them just the way they were. "If I pull them down," she pouted, "it changes the whole style of the dress."

"For the better, I assure you," Joe replied cheerily. "Now, be a good girl and walk toward me. Play to the camera."

Mandy did as instructed, tilting her chin up, keeping her gait slow and steady, like a model on the catwalk.

"Nice, nice," the photographer murmured. "Now, raise the dress up on one side so we can see some thigh."

I don't think so, she wanted to say, but didn't dare. Instead, she hoisted the hem a skooch. Enough to satisfy his "creative process."

"You're a natural, you know that?" Joe favored her with a smile. Mandy tried to gauge the truth in his eyes, this skinny dude with the soul patch and longish sideburns. "You're gonna go far in this industry, I can tell."

Mandy had longed to hear those words, yearned to hear them, rehearsed hearing them, her whole life. Back in the housing project, she'd stare into the mirror. There, she saw the classy, slim beauty inside the layers of childhood fat. She'd close her eyes and hear the fawning compliments, instead of the angry arguments between her parents on the other side of the apartment wall.

"I know talent when I see it, sweetheart, and you're the real deal," Joe reiterated.

So why wasn't she tingling with delight right now?

Joe came up to her and ran his fingertip across her shoulder blade. If he noticed her cringe, he didn't show it. "You're gonna be a big star one day. And you can take that to the bank."

Skeever put in, "Listen to the man. He's a star-maker."

Mandy tried to shake the unease, and the chills. "What other stars have you discovered?"

Joe grinned and stroked his soul patch with his thumb. "Not so sure you'd know their names—they changed 'em for showbiz—but you'd know their work if you saw it. You seen the movie *Double Trouble*? Or *Fly Me to the Moon*? Or *Ride 'Em High*?"

Mandy knew the name of every movie she'd ever seen. These weren't among 'em. Still, she tried to relax. Joe was a professional. He worked with Tim on the crew of *Skinny Dipping*, the big movie filming on Martha's Vineyard.

Tim had told her that photo gigs for aspiring actress-models were a side business for Joe. And he had connections. If these pictures came out well, he'd show them to the producer of *Skinny Dipping*, or, even better, to casting directors.

Mandy admitted, "I could do reality TV, you know, like as a stepping-stone to a career in movies."

Picturing herself as the next Bachelorette, maybe America's Next Top Model, both of which she totally qualified for, Mandy only half heard Joe respond, "Reality TV? I dunno. Videos, *that* I can promise."

The studio was sparse, very little in the way of props or furniture. A raggedy plaid couch was set against an exposed-brick wall, and an aged cracked-leather beanbag chair sat under the one window. Joe decided to pose her in various positions on and around the chair, which Skeever moved to the center of the room. After half an hour of this, Mandy was growing bored, and colder. "Any chance we can raise the thermostat here?"

Joe shook his head and kept on shooting. "We need to keep the studio chilly."

Skever put in, "Might ruin the picture if you warm up too much, y'know?"

Mandy shivered. Asshole.

World Photos was located several streets off the main drag in Hyannis and, to Mandy's chagrin, up three flights of stairs. She'd had to lug all her own changes of clothes, makeup, and hair stuff since Tim had freakin' bailed on her at the last minute, citing a just-scheduled night shoot that apparently had required the services of the best boy.

She'd whined, begged, cajoled, even offered a special "reward" if he came with her, but Tim insisted she'd be better off, less introverted without him there. Which made no sense. Wasn't she more apt to really shine with a supportive boyfriend around?

"Look, angel. I introduced you to Joe—just like you asked me to. When the pitchers are done . . ." Mandy winced. Tim had many fine qualities. Pronunciation was not one of them.

"Joe's gonna show them around to the right people in the biz. This is gonna get you started, just like we said." He learned over and gave her a kiss, and cupped her breast. "Knock 'em dead, babe. You got what it takes."

Mandy was ready to change into another outfit, even though the photographer seemed perfectly content with the lime green ensemble. Citing the need for a bathroom break, she grabbed her tote, along with a few of the clothes she'd brought, and headed to the ladies'. As she slipped out of the dress and reapplied her makeup, her cell phone went off. Had to be Tim, saying he was on his way back after all. With her free hand, she fished it out of her purse.

"Sarah?"

"Doesn't live here anymore." Mandy didn't hide her disappointment or annoyance.

Beverly Considine laughed. "I'm sorry. Mandy. How are you?"

"Kinda busy, Bev. Can I call you back later?"

"You can, but you know as well as I do that you won't. Look, Sar . . . Mandy, this is important. It's about Mitch."

Sighing, Mandy tucked the phone under her chin, freeing her hands to twirl her hair into an up-do. From outside the bathroom door, she heard Joe call, "Tick, tock, c'mon Mandy, we're waiting."

"I'm in the middle of a photo shoot, Bev. I'll call you when I'm done."

"I haven't been able to reach Mitch, and I'm really worried that something's up with him."

"Is that what your Spidey sense tells you?" Mandy cracked.

"Don't be cruel," Bev reprimanded her. "It's what my twin sister sense tells me."

"Sorry," Mandy apologized. She doubted if Mitch had shared the disastrous details of the robbery with his sister.

"Call Mitch," Beverly urged. "You have his cell phone, right? Just call him and tell him to call me. Tell him I'm really worried about him."

"Got the number programmed in," Mandy assured her. "I'll call as soon as I'm done here."

Joe summoned her again. Mandy checked her look in the mirror, and satisfied, flounced out. Skeever leaned against the wall nearest the exit, Joe paced the room. Neither seemed thrilled by her new ensemble.

She, however, wanted a totally different look, one that said "casual hip," in case she was being considered for the part of a teenager in a TV show.

So she'd chosen low riders, accessorized with a chain belt, and a sparkly cami beneath a sequined shrug. "What do you think?"

Not much, by their dour expressions. Finally Joe said, "Ditch the half-sweater, lower the pants, and let your hair down. We'll try it."

Mandy frowned. If there'd been an actual stylist here at her session, she was sure her look would prevail. She hesitated, but Joe tapped impatiently on his wristwatch. "Time's a-wastin'. We got a lot of shots to get in."

Mandy took a deep breath and forced herself to think rationally. Who was she to act like she really knew from professional photo sessions, anyway? Wasn't like she'd ever done one before. Maybe this was exactly what they're like, not the slick, doctored-up behind-the-scenes photos in her glossy magazines. Besides, she scolded herself, eyes on the prize. She was here, tonight, for a reason. And it had nothing to do with how low her jeans were, or letch-a-lump over by the door.

"Okay, hint of a smile, now, just a tease," Joe cajoled, keeping an eye trained on the lens.

Teasing, she could do. Mandy pivoted and lavished her most excellent come-hither pose on Joe's camera. The one that whispered, "Hey, hottie. Yeah, *you*, with the paunch and the pencil holder. Hella yeah, I think you're sexy. Come closer and I'll prove it, baby."

It was a total act—well rehearsed, too.

Joe was spectacularly unimpressed. "No, honey, I didn't say turn your body."

"But you said a teasing smile," Mandy noted.

Exasperated, he sighed. "If you turn away from the camera, you miss the whole point."

"Yeah, and them points are some-a your best assets," Skeever added.

Mandy glared at him. But he only laughed.

After several rolls of film in her now dangerously low jeans, Mandy suggested another change of clothes. "For a more sophisticated look."

Joe put the camera down and feigned wiping his brow. "More outfits?"

There was the chill again, creeping up her spine. She played it cool. "I brought, like, a dozen."

Joe scratched his chin. "Didn't Tim explain what to wear?"

Her stomach began to churn, but she swallowed her mounting doubts. Smiling brightly, she said, "I know how this works. The pictures have to display different looks, so casting agents can visualize you in a whole variety of roles. You know, like, sultry, cute, romantic, serious, comedic, tragic."

A stony silence filled the room.

Then, a sickening smirk spread across Skeever's face. "We only want one look. And you got that down pat."

Infuriated, Mandy had to hold her tongue, lest she gave this subhuman a verbal whiplash he would not forget.

Joe clarified, "You won't be needing any of the clothes you brought."

"Why not?"

"Because we're ready to get serious now. And you'll find all the . . . costumes . . . you'll need in the closet." He nodded toward a door she hadn't noticed before.

Warily, Mandy strode over to it, trying to think positive. Maybe there really were class outfits inside. But knowing, in the way you sometimes just do, that that wasn't true. A peek inside was enough to know what they had in mind.

Hands on her hips, she swiveled to face Joe. "Uh-uh. No way. I'm a real actress. All I need is a chance to prove myself. And your pictures are the first step. I thought you were professional."

"Oh, that I am, darlin', that I am," Joe agreed, cocking his head.

Mandy's heart thudded so loudly, she could barely hear herself. "Then what's with the slut-lingerie in there?" she challenged. "What's that gonna do for my career?"

It wasn't the sneer Joe gave her as much as the nauseating guffaw that belched from Skeever's fleshy throat. "Oh, ain't that a juicy one," he finally managed after he finished laughing. "'What's it gonna do for my career?'" he mimicked cruelly.

Joe was suddenly all business. "Enough. Let's not play coy here. As you said, I *am* a professional photographer. And the photos we take today will most certainly advance your career. But how do you expect to get hired if you don't show us your real talent?"

"I don't know what you mean," Mandy lied, praying he didn't see her shaking, and already formulating an exit strategy.

Joe came up to her, took her hand, and led her toward the couch. Stiffly, she acquiesced.

"There's a lot of money to be made in . . . uh . . . acting," he explained gently. "Especially for someone with your looks. And if you let us do our job, we can help you get started." He reached out, ran his fingers through her hair. "Natural redhead, huh?"

Mandy flinched and leaped off the couch as if she'd been launched. She growled, "No way. This is so not what we agreed to. I'm outta here."

Skeever moved swiftly for someone of his girth. Suddenly behind her, in one swift motion, he pulled her camisole top down, exposing her strapless bra. Mandy kicked him—hard, and right in the crotch.

"Eee-yow!" he yelped, holding his privates. "You bi—"

But Mandy had raced across the room, was

within arm's length of her bag. In which her cell phone lay.

Joe was faster. He blocked her way. "We paid for the studio time," he said sternly, "and we will need some photos to sell to recoup our investment. I suggest you finish undressing, and let us get underway."

Skeever recovered, and grabbed her elbow. "And just for that little karate kid move, you're gonna have to give us more than a pose. In fact"—he leaned in so she could smell his letch-breath—"I hear you're a cocktail waitress. I'm hungry for my *whore* d'oeuvres. Joe, here, he's entitled to the main course."

Mandy was trapped. Joe was on one side of her, Skeever on the other, going for her bra.

The door banged open, and quickly slammed shut.

All three whirled. Tim! Mandy tried to rush to him, but Joe and Skeever held her back.

"Timmy, oh, baby!" Mandy cried with relief. "They're trying to—"

With a dismissive wave of his hand, Tim headed over—not to her, but to the closet?

Mandy was dumbfounded. Was she hallucinating? Why wasn't Tim coming to rescue her? Why was she still in the vise grip of the tawdry twins?

And then Tim, her supposed boyfriend-slash-hero, did the weirdest thing. He pulled something off the hanger and held it up. "You look good in this. Put it on."

Mandy nearly passed out. It was her teddy. Her black, lace-up teddy. Which she'd paid a week's salary for, which had been . . . oh shit . . . stolen. In the robbery. Mandy's stomach sank, and she started to hyperventilate. This couldn't be happening.

Tim balled it up and threw it at her. "Catch."

"Why are you doing this, Tim?"

"To help you, baby, of course. You want a career, don't you? You think porn stars are born? Course not. They have to work hard for the money. You like working hard—I know that from experience," he snickered.

The color, what was left of it, drained from Mandy's face. A voice played in her head: Mitch's. "You're an actress: so *act*." She might not get an Oscar, but if she succeeded, she might get away unharmed.

Game on.

Mandy forced herself to laugh. "Um, well, okay, I guess I do understand now. I mean"—she faced Joe—"Now that Timmy's here, I guess it's all right. He's my man. . . ." She nearly vomited, saying that. "And he knows what's best for me."

She must've been better than she thought. Joe and Skeever let her go. And Mandy shimmied into Tim's arms. Pressing herself against him, she whispered in his ear, "You should have told me, baby. This whole thing took me by surprise."

"You never were the brightest," he said testily. "Now go be a good girl, pick up your Victoria's Secret special, and put it on."

At that moment, Mandy knew that if she ever got the chance, she would kill him. And it would not be a pretty, or easy, death. She retrieved the teddy, fetched her tote bag, and flounced—practice made perfect, after all—toward the ladies'. "Be right back, gentlemen."

"Not so fast." Joe's voice. "You won't be needing your bag in there. Hand it over."

Fear washed over her, but she shook it off. "My makeup's in there, I need to freshen up."

Joe rolled his eyes. "No, your cell phone's in there. Like I said, hand it over."

Mandy's legs turned to jelly. As she closed the bathroom door behind her, she struggled to breathe. There were no windows in here. How could she escape?

Then, she spied the sink where she'd been standing when Beverly Considine had called. She'd left the cell phone on the basin top. With a silent, yet fervent, prayer of thanks to the Considine clan, she punched in the number eight: the one Mitch had programmed in for her, to reach him in an emergency. There wouldn't be much time—seconds, at most—and no question, they'd be listening outside the door. She had to be smart: she text-messaged the address of World Photos, and this: "There's three of them. Hurry!"

And then she prayed. Hard.

When Mandy emerged from the ladies' room, she did the finest bit of acting in her limited career so far. She focused, and pictured the three thugs as her audience instead of her captors. In the mirror of her mind, *they* were naked and cowering. Lowlife Joe, all pale and concave, unequipped to please a woman, no doubt. Fatty-rat Skeever wasn't hard to imagine: all blubbery, hairy, and quivering. And then there was Tim—well, she knew him well enough. He'd already exposed himself for what he was: a small-time, no-talent, double-crossing hustler.

What a trio! What a joke. If she weren't in so far over her head, it'd almost be funny. Mandy had one goal right now: distract them, keep them busy, keep them at bay. She had to give Mitch time to get there. If it meant nude pictures, it'd be shameful, but nothing to compare to the hurt they could inflict on her.

In her lace teddy Mandy went to work, not only taking the directions Joe gave her, but playfully suggesting a few poses of her own. She had to make them believe she was down with this. That she could simply adjust all her red-carpet dreams to the sleaze-fest they had in mind. It seemed to be working. Jim snapped away exultantly, and Tim and Skeever played bookend voyeurs. Each moment that passed brought Mitch one moment closer. Mandy absolutely trusted that to be true.

Finally, Joe stopped clicking away.

"Reloading?" she asked, hoping to engage him in some stalling chitchat.

"You could put it that way," he said, motioning to Skeever. "Why don't you help the little lady into her next . . . costume?"

"Or," Tim chortled, "out of it."

The thug lunged toward her, and Mandy lost it. Lost her actorly concentration, lost her cool. Just as Skeever clamped a sweaty paw over her mouth, she extended her forefinger and middle finger and thrust them harshly into his eyes—a disabling motion that allowed her to scream at the top of her healthy set of lungs.

When the door burst open, the three stooges were taken completely by surprise, and by an enraged Mitch coming at Skeever, just like in the old days, fists first, and furiously flying.

Joss, right behind him, took on Joe with a well-placed left hook. And in a scene more surreal than when she'd been stoned and watched *2001: A Space Odyssey*, Harper, Ali, and Katie went for Tim.

"No, he's mine," Mandy cried. "Let me at the bastard."

Ali was all over it—all over Tim, that is. She sat on the skinny, squirming worm while Harper held his legs down and Katie pinned his arms.

And with all the pent-up rage of an accumulated nineteen years of feeling shafted, Mandy whaled on her betraying rat-bastard of a "boyfriend." She punched, and she kicked, and she clawed, and she cursed, and she never once let him see her cry.

And later, when the police had come and gone, when the toxic trio had been hauled off to the clinker, the housemates of 345 Cranberry Lane piled into Mitch's car and went home. After they'd pulled into the gravel driveway, Mitch asked the others, would they mind? He needed a private moment with Mandy. He folded her in his arms and allowed his childhood friend to finally break down. "Mitch," she croaked, "I don't know what I would have done if you hadn't been there."

Mandy had been humiliated in every way a girl could be, exploited, shamed, and pawed—but thanks to pluck, luck, and mostly Mitch Considine, the worst had not happened. Still, Mitch fretted over her like a mother hen. She almost laughed when he pleaded, "Will you talk to the girls, at least?" He thought she might confide in them. Right.

It was the only way Mandy could get him to

agree to get some sleep—it was nearly two in the morning! So after a long, hot, cleansing shower, she sat on the floor of her room, gratefully wrapped in Ali's large terry-cloth robe, and surrounded by the other girls. Ali toted mugs of decaf tea, and a basket of what she called "comfort munchies."

Mandy searched each one of their faces: cocoa-colored Harper with the clear blue-gray eyes; compact Katie, with the little girl bow lips and mind like a steel trap; and round, dark, easy-does-it, motherly Alefiya. At various times during the summer, she'd sneered at all of them. She'd been contemptuous, she'd been downright mean. Yet when she got into trouble, every one had come to her aid. No one had said, "Screw her, she deserves whatever happens."

Had the tables been turned? If Katie, or Harper, or especially Ali, needed to be rescued, would Mandy have bothered? A lump formed in her throat. She was not about to let it stop the words from coming. "I owe you guys, big time. I screwed up."

"What happened?" Katie asked. "I don't understand how you got into that . . . situation."

Harper shushed her. "You don't owe *us* an explanation. We're just relieved you're okay—and . . ." She paused to chuckle. "And not for nothing? You gave that asshole what he had coming. Righteous kick to the groin, dude."

The others laughed, which made Mandy tear up. "It was my fault."

"No way," Harper countered hotly. "Just because you were gullible enough to believe the photo session was on the level doesn't give anyone the right to exploit you."

Mandy focused on the threadbare carpet. "It was my fault the house was robbed."

Silence.

Finally, Ali said, "But you didn't plan it. I got there the same time as you, remember? You were completely freaked out."

"I made Tim a key," she confessed. "That slimeball. He tricked me, used me, and even left me a clue—taking my lingerie? And my scrapbook? I should have realized it was him, making fun of me all the time."

More silence.

She turned a tear-stained face to Alefiya. "I let them blame you."

Ali shrugged. "It's okay."

Mandy shook her head furiously. "It is *far* from okay. The whole summer I treated you like shit. I was such an asshole. And I'm so, so sorry."

Katie was curious. "Can I just ask, maybe this is a stupid question. But I wondered why you picked on Ali. What'd she ever do to you?"

"Simple." Ali surprised everyone by answering

for Mandy. "Every time she saw me, she saw herself—the way she used to be."

Mandy's jaw dropped. "You . . . you knew that all along?"

"I knew you weren't a racist. And your body language, the way you hold yourself, the way you—"

"Preen?" Harper put in.

Katie giggled.

Mandy flushed. "I was a fat kid, a really fat kid. 'Six-ton Sarah,' they called me. Sarah—that's my actual given name," she confessed. "Or 'Fatty Fat, the Gutter Rat.' I was this little flabalanche with big dreams of being slinky, of being gorgeous, of being admired. No one took me seriously. Except—" She paused.

"Mitch," Harper finished. "You guys grew up together, didn't you?"

Mandy nodded. "Only we hadn't seen each other for years. His sister—you know he has a twin, Beverly?—ran into me at McDonald's, and told me Mitch was looking for renters for the share house."

"You didn't want any of us to know you grew up together?" Ali said.

"Force of habit. Neither of us really wants to be reminded of the circumstances," Mandy conceded. "We were raggedy housing project kids. Mitch had brains, he studied his way out. Me? Not so much."

Harper said gravely, "I have to ask you guys a

question. It's really serious. It's like, if you know something that will hurt someone else, really rip their guts out, do you tell them? You know it's for their own good. If they like, live through it."

Mandy eyed her, nervous suddenly.

Ali said, "Sounds like this is about someone we know."

"It's about Mitch."

Harper inhaled sharply and unloaded. The housemates reacted predictably. Katie was shocked, stunned, disbelieving. Ali was near tears.

It was Mandy whose slow burn exploded like an earthquake. It was Mandy who went, to put it mildly, bat shit. It occurred to each of them, independently, that a restraining order—to keep Mandy away from Leonora— might not be a bad thing.

# Hang On, Harper—
# Katie Coughs Up a Truth Ball

"Seriously, mom, I'm *fine*." Harper let her mother babble on, all the while keeping her legs moving, eyes on the narrow trail ahead of her.

"No, I don't want to come home early. I'm gonna finish out the summer. There's only a week left, and I'm not just leaving the kids at camp," Harper reminded her mother.

She was thinking of Grace Hannigan, the camper whose dad had the affair with Leonora. Her family had been ripped apart after that, and these days, Grace clung to her counselor for dear life. No way Harper could abandon the kid, no matter what. Not that she wouldn't have liked to come home, she was so over the reason she'd left. A Luke sighting would be as meaningful as a cockroach sighting.

Sometimes? She saw the benefits of not being so close with your mom. Susan always intuited if something was wrong—and did her best to console and comfort her, which in Susan-world translated to: talking about it. Lots of talking about it.

No matter that Harper was hundreds of miles away, and could handle things on her own. Or that Harper'd had, like, enough yapping this summer to last a lifetime.

Her hair was up in a scrunchie, and the last rays of the day's sun tickled her neck. She pedaled eastward, back toward the share house. "Okay, Mom. Yeah, I really gotta go now. Bye. Yeah, love you too."

Harper pulled the hands-free earphone out and flipped the phone shut.

In the days following the stealth Luke attack, and the whole Mandy-goes-confessional-drama, Harper had taken frequent bike rides after work along the old railroad tracks, now converted to a bike trail. With each upward pedal-push, she'd chastise herself for being such a stupid little fool, falling in love with someone like Luke. With each downward push, she'd strengthen her resolve to not let it happen again. She ought to have known better. Shit, she did know better! "Won't Get Fooled Again"—wasn't that the classic Who song? Right on, bro.

As for Joss Wanderman? He'd arrived in her life bearing gifts of music, gifts of the soul. Sucks for you, dude, she thought. You're not getting in.

Cutting out after work served a purpose beyond a mind-rewind. Harper got to keep her distance from Katie, who was like an annoying Chihuahua chasing the bottom of Harper's pants. Katie just kept tugging at her, trying to "explain things."

Explain my tush! Like she cared to hear why Katie had really lashed out at her, why she'd allowed the backstabbing Lily to visit. She and Katie had coexisted all summer, even pulled together to help Mandy. They'd return to Trinity, and Katie would probably go back to treating her like she didn't exist. That'd be fine.

By the time she returned to 345 Cranberry Lane, the sun had set. Neither Mitch's nor Joss's rental car was in the driveway. She hoped Katie, still dating Natey, might be gone for the evening too.

No such luck. Instead, she found her roommate the only one home. Perfect time to pounce, which the platinum princess took full advantage of; woeful doe eyes included, free of charge. "Please, can we talk now? You have to believe me, Harper. I had no clue Lily would show up—let alone bring Luke!"

"Whatever." Harper wheeled her bike through the kitchen toward the basement door.

Katie followed, even as Harper guided the bumping two-wheeler down the steps. "You have to understand," she whined, "Lily wasn't supposed to even know where I was! I've been ignoring her phone calls and e-mails all summer. I didn't want her, or anyone, to find me *here*."

Harper nudged the kickstand, set the bike against the wall, and tried not to be intrigued by that last little nugget. Too bad she actually was, and Katie caught on quickly.

Besides, she was hungry, and intuitive Katie flipped open her cell phone and—before Harper could decide what to do—was saying, "Is this Mystic Pizza of Hyannis? I'd like to order a large pie, half veggie, half pepperoni, a Dr Pepper, and, hold on." She turned to Harper. "What do you want to drink?"

A half hour later, the two sat cross-legged on the living room floor, hunched around two upside-down wooden crates Joss had brought home that served as the coffee table.

Still, Katie used silverware to daintily cut her pizza slice into bite-size pieces on a real plate. Harper eschewed utensils, just folding a slice whole and devouring it, letting the cheese drip where it may.

"So, look," Katie said, "what I'm about to tell you is very, very private. You have to swear you won't tell anyone."

Only because she was mid-chew did Harper not retort, "And yet? I'm willing to bet it's very, very superficial and insipid." Wiping her mouth, she went with the gentler, "So why are you sharing now?"

Katie hesitated. "Maybe I care what you think of me."

Right. Maybe George W. Bush will learn to pronounce "nuclear."

"And maybe," Katie continued, sipping at her soda, "I care that you got hurt because of me. Is that so hard to believe?"

"Pretty much," Harper acknowledged, slurping spring water from the bottle.

That wasn't entirely true. Even *she* had to admit Katie'd displayed some true grit, especially that night they all schlepped to that godforsaken warehouse to rescue Mandy. Being a stuck-up Boston blue blood hadn't sucked up her soul. Not entirely, anyway. Still, Harper was wary of Katie's confession motivation.

"C'mon, cut me some slack. If I explain stuff, maybe you won't hate me so much. Besides . . ." Katie drew a breath and closed her eyes. Like even she couldn't face what she was about to say.

"Yeah?" Harper prompted.

"I could use a friend. I don't seem to have very many."

Harper knew she should just shut up and let

Katie vent. Sarcasm trumped manners. "What about Lily-the-boyfriend-slayer? Is the vapid vixen no longer on the VIP list for your debutante ball?"

"Harsh." Katie's voice broke.

What? Katie, on the verge of . . . an actual tear? Harper would not have thought her capable. Pinched by a twinge of guilt, she concentrated on her pizza slice.

Katie's eyes misted. "For one thing, there probably won't be a debutante ball."

The crust nearly flew from Harper's mouth. It was all she could do to keep from bursting out laughing. Oh, no! Poor Katie-pooh. No deb ball? This was The Kick's big trauma?

"I don't have any money. I'm not sure there's enough to make it through Trinity next year."

Intriguing, thought Harper. "Okay, I'll play. Where's all the moolah? Mom and Dad cut you off or something?"

A tear slid from Katie's manga-like eyes. "Not Mom. She doesn't even know."

"Know what?"

Katie pushed her plate away and cut a glance toward the door. "My father made some bad deals at the bank. He's being indicted for fraud."

Whoa. Serious stuff.

"When it happens," Katie continued, "it's all over. The money will be gone, the house seized, everything—my trust fund, college savings—my credit cards totally cut off. It'll be very public, all over the TV. Everyone will know."

Harper lost her appetite suddenly. Is that why Katie-bird had ended up in this dump? She asked, "Is it going down this summer? Is that why you're here?"

Katie tensed. She swiped her plate off the makeshift coffee table and started to get up, but changed her mind, set it down. "It hasn't happened yet. My parents are on a cruise, and Lily told me the staff is still running the house. I don't know when it's going to happen, only that it will."

It's like, thought Harper, when you blink your eyes and everything blurry turns painfully sharp and clear. Like a code unscrambled, a stuck-between-stations radio dial finding a clear signal, a missing puzzle piece found. A picture formed, neither pretty nor cool, and least of all "Kick-y."

Katie lifted her chin. She didn't appreciate being pitied. "This was supposed to be my summer to deal, to salvage my life. With Lily's help, I would've figured something out. I'm sure of it."

Ouch. One-two punch. First her dad blindsides her, then her flinty friend bails. Harper almost felt sorry for her. No wait . . . Harper *did* feel sorry for her.

Until Katie answered. Harper's carefully worded, "I'm not doubting you, but how can you be sure of all this?"

Turned out—hello!—to be the way Katie uncovered all sorts of dirt, including how she knew the history between Luke and Harper. She spied, eavesdropped, read people's journals, and in this case, hacked into her dad's private computer files. "My whole life is over," Katie whined.

To Harper? It seemed like Katie's *parents'* lives were, in fact, the ones taking a dive. Katie wasn't thinking about them. All she cared about was resuming her rockin' life as queen bee of Trinity High. The imminent downsizing of her social-slash-economic status clashed with her life plan.

So, ladies and gentlemen, Katie-acolytes of all ages, mused Harper, we can do the one thing The Kick cannot do: hack it when reality bites, when the going gets genuinely tough.

Katie was trying, though.

She detailed Plan Awesome for Harper. While living the high life in Lily's aunt's freebie mansion, they'd be piling up coin, earned by the counselor job, tips, plus what Katie could scam off rich boyfriends. If "the fraud thing," as Katie called it, didn't go down anytime soon, she could make it through most of her senior year at Trinity, head held high. No one in school would be the wiser.

Then, she could split, pay her own way to college if she had to, and not be around when shame came down on the House of Charlesworth.

And if it happened before high school graduation? Maybe, Harper offered naively, Katie could get a scholarship, financial assistance for senior year? The school, she knew well, was generous with that sort of thing.

Katie was shocked, stunned, furious at the temerity of the suggestion. "Are you kidding? Are you insane? Me—an object of pity? People looking down their snooty noses at me? What are you thinking?"

I'm thinking that karma is real. That you've spent the past three years sneering at "pitiable" people, at the losers, the feebs, the "fringe." You can dish it out all right, but the prospect of being on the other end is unfathomable. This is the petty world you created at Trinity, or at least perpetrated. I'm thinking this is pretty much justice.

Harper wasn't dumb enough, or mean enough, to say that to Katie's face.

Katie whined on mournfully. "Our house is as good as gone. If it happens while I'm at Trinity, I'll have to go live in some apartment or something. And everyone will know."

"So, that'd be the worst of it?" Harper dared inquire, picturing the cozy crib she and her mom shared.

Katie's face got very, very red. "What part of all this don't you understand? I will not have my entire life ruined because my stupid father turns out to be a thief! I've worked too long and too hard. I deserve the best clothes, the best crowd, the best"—she fumbled, pausing to think—"accessories!" she finally blurted.

Harper was astonished. You really could not overestimate Katie's superficiality.

Warming to her subject, Katie's whining intensified. "I deserve to make my debutante ball, to wear Vera Wang to the prom, to show up with someone worthy, in college and rich, like Brian or Nate. This is my senior year! I refuse to let my parents' shame be mine."

Snap! *That* was the moment Harper stopped feeling sorry for Katie. She had to ask, "What about your mom? She knows nothing?"

"She lives in perma-denial." Katie waved dismissively.

"So you'd just abandon her? When the thing goes down, you'd skip out?"

"Maybe I can rack up enough credits to get into college early—or something—I am so outta that scene. Whatever it takes, really."

"Your mother would be alone," Harper couldn't help pointing out. "It doesn't sound like coping is her strong suit."

Coldly, Katie responded, "She's never had to cope. She's all about the lifestyle, and it hasn't failed her."

"Knock, *knock*!" Harper said sharply, banging her fist down on the crate. "Mirror, mirror on the wall, who's the most deluded of them all? You have no respect for your own mother, yet you're all about following in her Manolos. Socialite, heal thyself!"

"You're mocking me?" Katie challenged. "You think this is some trite thing? You think it's no big deal?"

"That's the saddest part, Katherine. I think it *is a* very big deal. And the way you're reacting to it? Makes you as shallow and self-serving as any human being who's ever pranced across the planet."

**24**

Cape Cod

# *Katie's Got a Sinking Feeling*

The Kick's knee-jerk reaction was to kick herself for confiding in Harper. The frizzy-haired freak wore her fringe label like some badge of honor. Katie's first impression of Harper had not changed a whit all summer.

Except for this: what Harper had said to her? It *killed*. Killed in the way only the truth can.

"Denial much?" she asked herself as she furiously scrubbed the dishes in the kitchen sink—a few were her own, but never-thoughtful Ali had left an impressive pile of pots, plates, and silverware. How sad was it that Katie welcomed even this diversion? She didn't bother putting rubber gloves on.

That was supposed to be a bonding conversation with Harper. Katie had finally decided maybe Harper could help her. Her whole confession should have drawn her quirky roommate to her side! But no! Like everything with that girl, it had turned into a confrontation. Much as Katie took pains to explain, Harper stubbornly refused to see things her way.

Okay, so maybe Katie lost her cool more than once, maybe her voice betrayed her frustration. "You don't get it!" she'd railed at Harper. "Why would you? Unlike you, I'm *someone* at Trinity. I've earned the crown of homecoming queen and prom queen. I'm going to an Ivy League school, and then I will marry very, very well. I refuse to let anything change that."

But Harper had only cracked, "So your goal in life is to become a Desperate Housewife, a total cliché."

"No!" Katie had countered, kicking the cabinet beneath the sink now. "I won't be my mother. I'm the smart one. I won't be hoodwinked."

How could she think someone like Harper would get her? No matter how much Katie tried to make her see the righteousness of her cause, Harper was like a broken record. "What about your mother?"

"What about her?"

"Don't you think she'd need you?" Harper stared with those unnerving gray-blue peepers.

"Need me? What could I do for her?" Katie had shot back.

"You could be her daughter. You could be supportive. Besides, you're the brilliant Charlesworth,
you know how to cope. Why not use some of that
kick-ass talent when it counts?"

Katie's bow lips formed a straight line. "Save the
Disney Channel schmaltz for some naïf," she'd
advised Harper. "My mother boarded her private jet a
long time ago—and the cabin doors have closed. It's
too late to go all 'me and mom against the world.'"

Harper just kept shaking her head. "You're a
piece of work, Katie Charlesworth,"

"You think I'm horrible."

Harper's response cut. "I think you've been so
busy spying on other people, you haven't taken
time to figure yourself out, and what's really best for
you—the real you."

Katie'd countered miserably, "You still don't
understand. When it happens, I won't be able to
face anyone—Lily, the kids at school."

"That doesn't matter. As long as you can face
yourself. Can you?"

She stared into the sparkling clean, albeit
stained and cracked, porcelain sink. That was a
question Katie could not answer.

It was late when Katie returned to the share house.
She'd borrowed (without asking) a pair of Harper's
broken-in sneakers and had trolled the neighborhood,

circled the tiny boxlike houses, noted the (eww . . . ) cheap cars parked in neat driveways, and observed, when the window shades weren't drawn, the other residents of Cranberry Lane.

She'd never thought about them before—just random Cape Codders whose lives would never intersect with hers. Now, she was facing the possibility of being one of them. How did you even do that? Katie wondered. What do you do if you're without credit cards, designer duds, Escalades, and cool parties? How could you live in a house like this, so cramped you'd be too ashamed to invite anyone over. She couldn't wrap her brain around it.

Lily understood the terror Katie felt.

Harper did not.

Katie wasn't finished trying to force Harper to get it.

No cars were in their lame excuse for a driveway, which meant Mitch and Joss were out, but Ali was obviously home, evidenced by her pilly sweater on the floor by the staircase. If Mandy was around, you'd know it. Katie didn't hear her.

Katie marched into the room she shared with Harper, found her sitting up in bed, reading by the lamp on her night table. She'd meant to say something deep, to force Harper to understand what she was going through. But all that came out was, "What are you reading?"

Harper held the book up. *The Color Purple*, by Alice Walker.

"Any good?" Katie asked, not having heard of it.

Harper closed the book and drew her knees to her chest. "Did my sneakers fit you?"

Katie said sheepishly, "I didn't think you'd mind. I took a long walk, and I didn't have anything appropriate. Turns out we're the same size."

"Who'da thunk it?" Harper quipped. "So, what do you want?"

Katie twined her fingers and stretched her arms out. "I said I needed a friend. Why can't you just be one?"

"I assume this is your normal strategy—if you don't get what you want, or like what you hear, you just keep at it."

Katie smiled at her ruefully. "It's worked in the past."

Harper couldn't suppress a grin. "And yet? You need to be so over the past. We both do."

Katie smiled—maybe Harper was warming to her after all. "Lily and Luke?" she dished. "Just so you know? They deserve each other. If your ex really is into her, he's headed for a crash-and-burn. Lily's wicked, already planning on kicking him to the curb. And if you take him back"—Katie wagged her finger at Harper—"you're a fool."

Harper widened her eyes. "Never. But—whoa,

why would I take advice from you? Do you even like the guys you've been going out this summer?"

Katie considered. "Not Brian, he turned out to be a bore. Nate? Maybe. He's got the whole kindness vibe, and he wears it well. But I don't . . . exactly see . . . the two of us together. No matter what happens."

"So basically, you're just using him, too," Harper concluded.

"God, Harper, everyone uses everyone. How do you not know this by now?" She flung back her head, exasperated.

"I won't—can't—believe that."

"Oh right. You believe in love for its own sake. Oh, wait, didn't that get you in trouble already?" Katie gave her long look. "You're going to do it again, aren't you?"

Harper's eyes flashed dangerously. "What are you talking about?"

"Joss. You're crazy in love with him. It's totally obvious."

Harper abruptly switched off the bedside lamp. "Darkness falls. Night-night, roomie."

"There's something you might want to know about him," Katie said.

Harper flipped the light back on.

At that exact moment, a voice startled both of them. "What, Katie? What would she need to know about me?"

Katie whirled around, Harper sat straight up.

From the doorway, Joss took a tentative step into their room. "You're about to tell Harper that I'm not who I say I am? That I've deceived her?"

"What are you doing here?" Harper and Katie said as one.

"I live here, don't you remember? So go on, tell her," he goaded Katie.

From the day she'd first seen Joss Wanderman, standing in the doorway of the share house—not unlike his studied-casual pose right now—Katie knew she knew him from somewhere. It'd come to her, she'd been sure of it. And then just the other day? Two and a half months later? It had.

It was from a feature article in the society section of the *Boston Globe Sunday* magazine. About J. Thomas Sterling, one of the richest businessmen in the country, a savvy venture capitalist who'd built an empire to rival the Trump Organization. Many times married and even more sought after, J. Thomas wielded power like an ax, using and abusing it to cut down his enemies and threaten those who might be. The only reason she'd happened upon the article was that Lily had e-mailed it to her, suggesting she check out the "number-one son" in the article's family portrait. "Josh Sterling," she'd written, "*Apprentice* material, hottie, and available. Someone to meet, don'tcha think?"

The photo, maybe two years old, showed a young collegiate, conservative and preppy, short brown hair, wearing an argyle sweater under a Zegna sports jacket. Patriarch J. Thomas was smiling broadly, his arm around his son's narrow shoulders. Joss—or Josh—looked massively uncomfortable. Like he'd rather be—

"Anywhere but there." Joss was telling his story to Harper. "That life was never what I wanted. So I split, stayed under the radar, haven't looked back."

"I take it," Harper speculated, "your father wasn't exactly down with the music thing." She nodded at the guitar Joss held.

"Not so much," Joss confirmed. "I'm the only son, heir to the throne. I'm supposed to ascend, run the organization, not haul equipment in exchange for getting to play backup for—"

"Does your father know where you are?" Katie interrupted.

Joss had been staring at Harper, trying to gauge her reaction to the exposé, but he switched his attention to Katie. "I'm sure. J. Tommy has the resources to find anyone. I'm guessing he's lying back, giving me my space—confident I'll come crawling back."

"Will you?" The question came again, from both girls.

Clutching the neck of his guitar, Joss sank slowly

onto Katie's bed, the unoccupied one. "A month ago? Two months ago? I would've said never. No way, José. Keep the money, drive the limos off a cliff, I don't need any of the perks. To quote an old rock guy, 'It ain't me, babe.'"

"And now?" asked Katie cautiously. "You would go back? Did something change?"

Joss had returned to trying to read Harper's face. But she wasn't giving it up. He lifted the guitar into his lap, flicked his fingers across the strings. "A lot has changed, actually, in the past three months."

Katie crossed her legs and shifted her position. Harper remained still. She wondered if Harper hated Joss for lying, for deceiving her about his background. She wondered if Harper had been waiting for something like this, something she could use to convince herself that Joss was just another Luke, an unworthy jerk.

Joss finally said, "I didn't mean to deceive you."

An expression crossed Harper's face, and Katie read it perfectly. She was more in love with him than before!

"You didn't deceive anyone," Harper confirmed. "I think we all got to know who you really are this summer. I think that's what you wanted all along."

Deep, Katie thought. And then wondered, what now? Will Joss unburden himself and tell Harper his other big secret? The not-so-worthy one? The one

Harper would find truly contemptible, and hurtful.

"There's something else you should know." Joss leveled his gaze at Harper. "Something I'm not proud of."

Katie jumped up, pivoted, and dashed from the room. He was gonna do it, stupid fool. She so didn't need to hear it.

Only, due to the thinness of the walls, the silence in the rest of the house, and—okay, if she had to admit it—her own keen interest, she heard everything.

Joss outed himself about sleeping with Mandy.

Harper outed her real feelings. Disgust, jealousy, rage. And now—the excuse she'd been looking for for cutting him off.

Joss fell all over himself explaining, apologizing, trying to make Harper understand that it had happened, and was over, before he'd realized his feelings for her. That he'd been a jerk.

Katie had to strain to hear the rest. From Harper, it sounded like, "Of course."

From Joss, it was all about, "I gave in to temptation, but then I met you. And no one tempted me after that. Harper, wait . . ."

The light went out in the room. Katie heard Joss's defeated footsteps heading away. Despite the darkness and the distance, she could absolutely read Harper's mind: close call.

25

Cape Cod

## She Rescued Him Right Back

Mitch's life flashed before him. Only not the way it's always described in books or shown on TV—that moment when you know you're dying. Not like a movie on rewind, or a comic book strip of halo-lit snapshots, and certainly not, as he'd heard more recently, a PowerPoint slide presentation in the great beyond, hitting on his accomplishments, defeats and goals.

He'd have chosen any of those above what was happening now! Mitchell James Considine's autobiographical death scene was coming at him as a rush of ocean waves—cold, overwhelming, disorienting, inescapable.

A scene would appear—he and Beverly, six years old, being chased by playground bullies—then, roar up in front of him like a Scooby-Doo monster with its claws extended, before simply curling in on itself and enveloping him.

One after another they came at him, relentlessly. The day his father, grizzled and drunk, kicked them out of the apartment. Mitch, at eight years old, scared and shaking, climbed up the fire escape, and snuck in through the window to let his mom and sister inside.

A moment in the puke-green school cafeteria, when third-grader Sarah Riley didn't have her food stamps, and chose to go hungry rather than let any-one know. Mitch gave her his sandwich, insisting he wasn't really hungry, anyway.

His lungs screamed and he couldn't breathe. He was so cold.

Next, the pants were too short, his red socks were sticking out, everyone was laughing at him. Splash! A wave of shame hit as he watched himself now, self-consciously crossing the stage to receive his high school diploma. He knew, but did not see, his mom in the back row of the auditorium, beaming with pride as he was named class valedictorian.

His arms strained, ached with the effort of keep-ing up with the waves. More were coming.

An image of his mom, returning home late, hag-gard from scrubbing other people's floors—the name DORA stitched to her gray uniform; the pinkie pact he'd made with Bev, swearing they'd get out of the projects, and then, from far away, another image was coming toward him. But who was that? A girl, her face blurred, because she was twirling like a ballerina, swirling around him, faster and faster, crashing down now and sucking him under.

"Mitch! Mitch! Can you hear me?"

He heard only in gasps and gurgles, "Mitch, I'm almost there!" He strained toward it, but it was too faint, and he was too far away.

"Mitch, I'm coming! Hang on!"

Who was coming? What could he hang on to?

The other swimmer! Instantly, Mitch flashed to the present. He was the lifeguard. And he'd seen someone out there, a child, arms flaying, needing him. How many times had the boy gone under? He remembered being panicked, scampering down the lifeguard post, racing into the water, and swimming out as far as he could. He thought he'd called out, "Where are you? Hang on, I'm almost there!"

He couldn't find the drowning swimmer. The boy was too little, and the ocean was too big; it was all too much. He was the lifeguard, and he was lost.

An innocent kid would die today, maybe had already. Because Mitch Considine hadn't been fast enough.

Another wave. But, unlike the others, this was just a white, foamy screen, no snapshot of his life appeared on it. This wave was far more powerful than the others, sucking him into blackness. So was this it, finally? He'd gone under for the last time.

Mitch felt a new sensation, something tough and sinewy, yet soft and familiar. If this was death, it was more comforting than he'd thought it could be. It felt like someone's arm—God's?—strong and sure, bent at the elbow, wrapping itself halfway around his chest, locking in under his armpit.

It was pulling him, tugging him, yanking him, even . . . not down, deeper into the cold, black pit . . . but up. Pulling him back.

"No, I have to save him. I have to save . . ." Mitch wanted to say, "Stop! Forget about me, there's a child out there who needs to be rescued first." But no words were actually leaving his mouth. It was dark where he was now.

Her lips were soft, lush. Not like Leonora's, whose kisses felt like little pecks, teasing, perfunctory, always leaving him wanting more.

Whoever was kissing him now *was* giving him more—

Breathing life into him.

He coughed. Blinked. He looked straight into the sun, and saw the outline of an angel, a halo suspended above long waves of copper hair.

"Mandy? Is that you? Are we . . . ? Wha . . . wha . . . happened?"

He heard someone, not her, respond, "She saved your life, man."

Other voices chimed in, so many that they overlapped each other, broke into one another, confusing him.

"How lucky can a guy get?" "Mouth-to-mouth from the hottest babe on the beach?" "Oh, man! It's like *Baywatch*, only real!" "You one lucky sumbitch, y'know?"

Mitch wanted to get up, but his head was too heavy to lift. He managed to turn his cheek onto the soft sand. Kneeling next to him was another lifeguard, Doug or Drug or something—Mitch had never been sure—seriously freaked. "Got here as soon as I could, Mitch," he panted, "you are lucky this chick was here. I wouldn't have made it."

This chick? He didn't mean Mandy? That wasn't possible. So who was she? Where was she? Mitch tried to turn his head the other way, but it was too much work.

Doug gripped his arm. "What made you go out there, man?"

To rescue a drowning swimmer, why else? He'd seen small arms waving, going down, being sucked under. Had he been hallucinating? "There wasn't . . . ?"

He coughed. "No one was drowning?" he finally spit out.

"Just you." Consciousness had returned fully. He'd know that voice anywhere. It matched the vision he saw, the haloed redhead. Mandy ran her fingers through his hair. Then she handed him a towel. "Here, blow your nose, you'll be fine."

Mitch exhaled and felt his body uncoil. He was safe now.

"Okay, show's over, you can all leave." Mandy booted the looky-loos, then whispered, "You fell asleep, you dumb lug."

"You were here?" Mitch asked stupidly. "I didn't see you."

"I was sunbathing next to the lifeguard station. I waved, but you were asleep, so I let you be."

"You should have woke me up," he said weakly. "It was irresponsible."

"Yeah, well, I made an executive decision," she cracked. "You needed your sleep more than I needed an even tan. I sat on the beach and took watch for you. No one was even in the water."

He felt like a total idiot. She confirmed it too. "Suddenly, you jerked up—probably in the middle of a nightmare—and you ran out there like your pants were on fire."

His throat hurt when he laughed. "Remember the time my pants really were on fire?"

It'd been back in the bad old days. Mitch, Bev, and Mandy were walking home from junior high school. They turned a corner and saw black pillars of smoke coming from the Dorchester Housing Projects. Turned out some lunatic on the fourth floor of their building had decided to make a bonfire of his ex-wife's apartment. Mitch had broken into a run, terrified that his mom might be trapped inside the burning building. Luckily, she hadn't been home, but he'd exited the building spewing smoke and fanning flames off his behind.

Laughing transformed her, he thought, brought back the bright-eyed freckle-faced kid he'd known, and maybe crushed on. Just a little. "I was always trying to be the hero," he admitted. "Old habits die hard."

"Yeah well . . ." She cut her eyes away from him, out to the ocean. "Some of us appreciated it. Still do."

It was a struggle, but Mitch pushed himself up on his elbows and grazed her fingertips with his. "I don't know what would've happened to me if you hadn't come."

Mandy shot him a rueful grin. "Died, I suppose."

Mitch grinned. She always did tell it like it was.

"I *told* you this was a bad idea," Mandy chastised him. "You're a great guy, and a hero, too, but you're not Superman."

"Cut me some slack, okay? I had no choice."

Mandy's face clouded. "There's always a choice, Mitch. Someone real smart told me that once. Mighta even been you."

Look where "real smart" has gotten me, he thought.

"Do you think," she asked, "it's this sickness people like us have? This obsession to have money, be famous? Do any stupid thing just so people will look up at us, instead of look down—like they did when we were kids?"

Not so long ago, Mitch would've been righteously offended at the trite suggestion, and the comparison of "Mandy Starr" and her hackneyed pipedreams with Mitch Considine and his lofty goals and worthy ambitions.

"We both made some real asinine moves this summer," he conceded, "trying for a better life than the one we had. I never thought it would be this hard."

She agreed, stroking his arm. "I worked like crazy to lose all that weight. I thought just by being sexy, like in the magazines, I could be a winner, you know?"

He did know. All too well. He, too, thought he could lose the scruffy little outside-looking-in boy; if he worked tirelessly, he could launch himself right into another life. Leonora's life. With effort, he put his arm around Mandy's shoulders, and together, they lay back down, her head resting on his chest.

"I knew better than to go to that photo studio. I knew it was a sleazy setup. But a part of me believed it would turn out the way I dreamed. The pictures would like, dazzle 'em. I would be famous, special. You know?" She tipped her chin up so she could look into his eyes.

He had to close them. Otherwise she'd know exactly what he was thinking: You *are* someone special. You always were.

Much later, he and Mandy sat outside, on the deck, a six-pack of beer and a bag of chips on the little table between their chairs. Mandy had managed to talk Mitch's boss into believing she and Mitch had been kidding around and things got out of hand. That this lifeguard—how ridiculous!—hadn't nearly drowned. That Mitch shouldn't be fired.

Funny, he was no longer sure he still wanted the second job, or even the tennis gig anymore. He'd been so single-minded all summer—hell, all his life, really—that to not be sure of something, to not have a goal, felt strange. And yet, it was less unsettling than he'd imagined.

He took a long slug of beer and eyed her. She'd put on an oversize football T-shirt and slipped into a pair of well-worn jeans. She was barefoot, and he noticed her toes; the sparkly pink polish reminded him of the first night at the share house.

He hadn't planned to ask, but couldn't help himself. "You didn't just 'happen' to be sunbathing, did you? You were keeping an eye on me, making sure I was okay. Weren't you, Sarah?"

She smiled ruefully. "Like you didn't just happen to program your cell phone into mine that first day? You wanted a way to save me—if I needed it."

Why this girl ever thought herself stupid was a mystery to him.

"Mitch?" Her voice was hesitant suddenly. "I *was* keeping an eye on you, but for more reasons than you thought. I knew taking on two jobs was gonna kill you. And"—she paused, uncharacteristically—"I was trying to find a way to show you that it wasn't worth it. That *she*"—another pause, pointed this time—"wasn't worth it."

That's when Mandy broke the news, told him what everyone at 345 Cranberry Lane already knew but had been afraid to tell him. Mandy told Mitch the truth about Leonora, exactly what Harper had seen last month.

She'd gone to Chatham herself, Mandy informed Mitch, sat in the grand foyer (she pronounced it foy-YAY) of the Quivvers mansion, told the maid she'd wait for Leonora to come home. "I had to confront her," Mandy explained. "I was gonna make her confess. I was gonna punch the slut out for cheating on you."

"But you didn't?" Mitch said quietly. He was hearing this from afar, it seemed, catching maybe every other word she said. It didn't matter. Mandy was to the point, and clear. She repeated exactly what Leonora had told her.

His sweetheart, his beloved, the woman he lived and almost died for, had been cheating on him all summer long. She felt guilty, sure, but not enough to stop! That's why she'd been so weird, so hard to get through to. Leonora had come to the share house that day to break it off, to tell him she was ending their relationship. But he hadn't let her get a word in edgewise, he'd been so busy showing her off, like his big trophy. And then she got so angry, she didn't want to talk to him at all!

It was right after that, Harper had caught her in bed with little Gracie's dad. That's when things got really complicated. Leonora had freaked out, didn't know what to do, or how to act. If Harper blabbed, her whole life would be ruined! The sad truth was that Mitch was only a small part of it. If Harper told, her parents would find out that their twenty-year-old daughter was having a sleazy affair with a married man—doing it in a hotel room?! No one did that sort of thing. Or if you did, you certainly didn't get caught! She was fairly sure her parents would've booted her out of the country somewhere.

Leonora didn't know how to handle it. She'd

spent every day trying to gauge Mitch, to guess what, if anything, Harper had told him. One minute, she'd be lavishing attention on him; the next, completely disengaged. Now Mitch knew why.

Yes, Lee admitted to Mandy, she did insist her father intervene with the cops, get Mitch off the hook so he wouldn't have an arrest record. At first, she'd truly thought the incident would serve to remind her how good she had it with wholesome, worthy Mitch Considine.

Just the opposite. It had only proved what Leonora had suspected: She was bored with Mitch, the knight in shining armor. She wanted out of the relationship, but didn't know how to end it.

Hours earlier, Mitch had been a drowning man. Now, he was into a serious beer buzz. Finally, everything was crystal clear to him. It would not ever matter how much money he made, what kind of career he'd forge, how big the ring would be that he'd give her as an engagement gift: Leonora was never going to be his.

Mandy held him as he sobbed. When it was over, when his tears had been spent, he couldn't say if they'd been tears of rage, regret—or relief.

# The Clambake: Everyone, Out of Your Shell!

### Katie

Hot, hot, *hot*! Katie was surprised the sand beneath her bare feet still burned. It was, after all, the end of August, just before sunset. Carrying a pot full of just-cooked corn on the cob, she had to do this run-and-hop thing (how graceful!) from the backyard deck toward her beach blanket buddies—Mitch, Mandy, Harper, Joss, and Alefiya—who were all digging in for an end-of-summer big-ass clambake.

Mitch had said it was "tradition," but Katie so doubted it. She suspected he wanted to start a new one.

As she neared the human hodge-podge she'd lodged with, she had to laugh. The hippie, the hussy, the prep, the slob, the slacker, and yeah, the princess (that'd be her)—they'd accused each other of all of the above—somehow, the whole crazy quilt had worked. Today, the end of their last day living together, they'd celebrate the against-all-odds friendships—and love affairs, even—that had resulted.

In the middle of the clashing array of beach blankets, towels, flip-flops, T-shirts, and shorts tossed on the sand sat a gi-normous steamer pot, courtesy of Clambakes-To-Go (no one wanted to risk Ali cooking: The house was clean!). The pot was full of orangey red lobsters, shrimp, clams, and oysters; next to it sat an uncharming plastic tub filled with clam chowder, and several smaller plastic containers with drawn butter, crackers, and horseradish-ketchup dip. A kid's beach pail was employed to hold nutcrackers, napkins, and paper cups—clambake accessories.

Ali had been put in charge of the music, and she'd toted a ghetto-blaster and stack of CDs to the party, which Katie was sure could be heard all the way to Chatham. Already, Ali was up and dancing, singing into a beer bottle-cum-microphone, "And I . . . yi . . . yi . . . yi . . . will always love . . . you-ou . . . ou . . . ou . . . ou!" Her Whitney impression was wanting, but Katie'd heard and seen much, much worse.

Mitch, working food patrol, was "Langostino-man"—so dubbed by Joss, who (naturally) had taken on bartending chores. Taken them very seriously! Beyond popping beer-bottle caps, Josh was tending to blenders full of frothy frozen margaritas and daquiris; the upended crate they'd been using as a coffee table since the robbery now served as a bar counter, on which he'd lined up shot glasses as well. Impressive!

Katie trooped toward them, shouting, "Corn here! Getcha corn on the cob!" She set the pot and her rear end down on someone's SpongeBob blanket and buried her toes in the sand.

It'd been a head-spinning week. Lucky her day camp gig had ended the prior weekend; she'd needed the time to execute her new plan.

This one she'd dubbed Plan A—for Amends.

Katie had more than a few to make. In doing so, she began to feel like her old self again: The Kick, large 'n' in charge, doing what needed to be done. Her exceptionally stylish (always adorable) way.

The day Joss had delivered the news had turned the tide. That day, she should have been destroyed, debilitated, beyond consolation. Instead, she felt empowered. How weird was that?

Joss had come through, big-time, for her. He'd reached out to his own family, the deep-pocketed and deeply connected Sterling Organization. It hadn't taken them long to unearth the Charlesworth scandal secrets. They confirmed her worst suspicions. Richard Charlesworth would soon be charged with fraud. The FBI had been building a case, waiting to pounce until they had every last shred of evidence, an indictment assured. They'd allowed Richard and Vanessa to go on their summer cruise; agents would be waiting when the ship docked back at Boston Harbor in another ten days.

Devastating as the details were, knowing *when* it would occur was a huge relief. It allowed Katie to let that boulder of doubt and fear roll off her shoulders.

Joss had gone completely above and beyond informant. He'd offered her money. "As much as you need, to get you through school, and after."

She'd broken down and sobbed. Not for her parents—not yet, anyway—not for herself. In her life, Katie had not known that kind of generosity, and it touched her deeply. Joss didn't want anything from her.

Yet? She was going to do something for him all the same.

Later that day, she'd sought out Harper, lazily reclining on the living room floor. Harper'd propped a bed pillow up against the fireplace mantel, and, while she didn't look all that comfortable, she was less than thrilled to be interrupted from what Katie termed a marathon read-fest. To her knowledge, Harper had done no writing since the day Joss admitted his fling with Mandy. Lately, all Harper did was take long bike rides and read books. She must've gone through a dozen hardcovers in the last week.

"Do me a favor?" Katie had said. "Pick your head up from the world of fiction and listen to something real. You need to know what Joss just did."

"I don't need to know, and I don't really want to either," Harper corrected her. "I'm over it."

"Too bad," Katie replied, plopping down next to her and proceeding to fill her in on Joss's big-hearted gesture. Harper pretended not to care, but Katie had learned to read her roomie well enough by now. Harper was calculating what it had cost Joss to help Katie.

"He's not Luke," Katie kept repeating. "Joss is the real deal. They don't come around often. And"—Katie had put in before Harper could dismiss her—"he needs you."

"Not."

"You're not into his money—or his looks, even. You connect with him. The music thing—it's obviously what he's about. You get it. If he has to go back to Sterling, Inc., do you think anyone there will?"

Harper, stubborn as she could be, wasn't budging. At least not on the Joss topic. But, clearly, she was worried about Katie. "So it's really going down as soon as you get back to Boston? Before school starts?"

Katie nodded.

"If you want . . . ," Harper started, "I know I'm . . . what do you call me? Fringe! But if you want to stay at school, you can live with me and my mom. It's just an apartment, but it's big."

Katie smiled, and told Harper what she'd told Joss. She'd think about it. She had choices. She'd gotten something out of this summer she'd never expected: real friends. Who didn't give a hoot about The Kick, or what she could do for them. Harper, of all people, "fringe-girl," had forced her to examine exactly what it was she'd been so obsessed with holding on to. Her parents' life? How empty, and pathetic, was that? Look where it had gotten them.

Speaking of her parents, Katie had a responsibility, something she'd never ducked in all her life. Her mom, oblivious and flawed as she was, loved Katie as best she could. Vanessa needed her now. So Katie would go, stand by her, no matter where they ended up. Somehow, she would force herself to understand her father's side of the story too. That would come later.

As for the ridicule she would certainly suffer at the hands of the Trinity best-of-breed crew?

Bring it! They—Lily included—would meet the real Kick. She could, and would, deal. Without a credit card (pause for a real sob), if it came to that; without a debutante ball; without this season's designer best—with or without (she still hadn't decided) Nate Graham—but with her head held high.

Katie didn't have time to dwell on what would be. She did, however, have ten days until the news broke. Which meant she still had some clout on the Cape. She used it, one last time. As a favor to a housemate, who'd morphed into a friend.

His name was Whitford (really). He was freckled, friendly, sun-dappled, deep-pocketed—the real-life Kennedy kin she'd run into at Blend in Province-town. Whitford was ripe for summer fun, and very open to meeting someone, especially when Katie described her friend as cute, carefree, and fun-loving.

But a funny thing happened when she told Mandy that she'd set her up with Whitford—the Kennedy connection. The redhead, who'd taken years off when she removed her makeup, had said, "Thanks, but no thanks. I'm kinda happy with the catch I made on my own. Oh, BTW: Mandy doesn't live here anymore. The name is Sarah."

### Sarah

Sucking out the sweet meat from the tiny lobster legs was as delicious and satisfying as she'd always imagined. To Katie's "*Eeww*, no one eats that part of it," she'd laughed. "Now you know someone who does," she'd said, and cracked open another. Mitch took a slug of beer and draped an arm around her. Sarah did not think herself capable of this much joy. Funny that she should derive it from her fucked-up childhood, from the Considine twins, Mitch and Bev, friends she'd excised years ago, along with the excess poundage. If she were a literary type, like Harper over there, she might say she had reclaimed her soul this summer. But since she wasn't? She'd just let Joss pour her a frozen margarita and get up and show Ali, wiggling her bodacious booty to *The Best of ABBA*, what a real "Dancing Queen" looked like!

Sarah's soaring spirits had as much to do with the amends she'd made before leaving the share house. The first was a no-brainer. Hitching a ride with Mitch, she'd gone to the biggest pet store she could find, and picked up . . . jeez, who knew they even had special food for ferrets? Let alone ferret toys? Ali had been overjoyed, even though Sarah had stopped short of petting the thing.

On Katie's advice, and on Katie's cue, she then accosted Harper, who slammed her book down in frustration and demanded, "Does this bare living room look like a confessional to you? First Katie, now you, desperately needing to tell me something. What part of 'I don't care' don't you get?"

"A lotta stuff went down this summer," Sarah

had said calmly. "If not for Mitch, and the rest of you, I'd've been in deep shit."

Harper folded her arms over her chest. "We already had our sista-friend bonding session. Gratitude extended and accepted. End of saga."

"Not quite," Sarah contradicted. "Before we leave, I really want you to know that I'm not the same shit heel I was three months ago."

"Fine! I get it! You've seen the error of your ways. So, can I have the big bedroom now?"

"In your dreams." Sarah feigned annoyance. "But you can have something better: the truth. Your choice to accept it or not, but here it is: I threw myself at Joss. I totally . . . I don't even know why . . . he was there, he was easy on the eyes, he was unattached. I wasn't into him, and trust me, he was never into me. It was random sex. Okay, so when I found out he was on tour with some aging rock star, I thought he could hook me up. Y'know, introduce me to the manager, the agent, make some connection. But we never got that far. Joss ended it soon after it began."

Harper sighed. "So you sent Mandy Starr packing, and what, you're going all Amish now? You're withdrawing from the Amazing Actress-slash-Model Race?"

"Of course not!" sniffed Sarah. "I have talent, a gift. Why squander it? But I'm going to do it right:

take acting lessons, take it slow. And when I'm ready, sign up with a real agent. Legit. Mitch is going to help me."

Harper couldn't suppress a smile. "That's actually pretty terrific. He's an amazing guy."

"Yeah, so what am I? Liverwurst? Mitch *is* getting me—a big improvement over that prissy tight-ass Leonora," she asserted, sticking out her prodigious chest and tossing her wavy hair.

Harper laughed. "You go, sister."

Sarah lowered her voice. Earnestly, because this was really important, she said, "Listen, Harper. This isn't about me. I'm real sorry for the foul things I said this summer. And the worse things I did. But don't hate Joss because of me. That's a really dumb reason."

## Joss

When he'd picked up the phone and punched in his father's office, Joss wholly expected some administrative assistant to answer. He was ready to say, "Please put Mr. Sterling on the line."

But after several rings, turned out J. Thomas *was* on the line. "Son?" his voice borderline-quavered. "Is that you?"

Of course his father had probably tracked Joss's new cell phone number a year ago. "Yeah, Dad," he confirmed. "It's me. Joshua."

His father harrumphed. "Not Joss? Took me a while to get used to that"—affirming Joss's suspicions that his dad had known all along where he was—"but now I rather like it. Helps me see you in a whole different way."

"What way's that?" Joss held himself in check, trying not to let the old resentment get in the way. He was calling to ask a favor, nothing more. Irritating the old man wasn't the best strategy. He asked after his dad's health, his sister and brother, anything else he could think of before revealing what he really wanted.

J. Thomas Sterling went along with it. Not once did he bark, "What the hell did you think you were doing?" Or taking that superior attitude: "So, I see you've come to your senses." Or some other condescending thing Joss imagined he might throw at him.

Instead, his father listened. Said he'd be happy to do Joss the favor—it'd be easy for him to get information regarding Richard Charlesworth. And took the moment to remind his son that his bank accounts—dormant since Joss hadn't touched them—were, as always, being well invested, and available to him.

The true miracle, Joss reflected, was that J. Thomas never once asked the reason for the favor. Nor did his dad want to know when he was coming home, nor mention that the corner office designated for him still sat empty. Instead, he said haltingly,

"Son, it means a lot that you called. Every time the phone rang, I kept hoping it'd be you." Joss couldn't be sure if what he heard after that was the sound of J. Thomas Sterling, Esq., weeping. He wouldn't know what that sounded like.

The call had put him through the emo-wringer. But in a strange way, it gave him the courage to place another call, to another father. To ask another favor.

He was a little looped himself, when, pouring a second frozen margarita for Mandy—that is, Sarah—he felt someone come up behind him and slide an arm around his waist. Because it felt so sweet, and right, he didn't turn away.

"That was pretty amazing, what you did for Katie," Harper said, letting him wrap his arm around her shoulders. "You obviously told your dad where you were."

Joss laughed. "You make it sound like I turned myself in! Like I'm going to jail."

"Won't they expect you to work in the family business?"

"More than likely," he said, nodding.

"What about your music?" She stared up at him with those amazing light gray-blue eyes.

"What about yours, Harper Jones?"

She frowned. "When did we start answering a question with a question?"

Joss withdrew his arm from Harper's shoulders. "Let's get some oysters before they're all gone."

Harper pursed her lips. "Shrimp for me, oysters for you."

"That works too," Josh agreed, swiping a couple of beers and leading her to the outer edges of the clambake.

She peeled the shrimp gingerly, watching him slurp down the oysters indelicately. He handed her a beer. "You wouldn't rather a frozen drink, would you?"

"No way. I'm not about the hard liquor—learned my lesson at the party."

He laughed. "Don't remind me."

She kicked him, gently. And he fell more deeply in love with her. Which is precisely why he had to risk it: "So, I ask you again, Ms. Jones, what about your music? When are you going to deal with it?"

Harper sighed, like she'd expected this. And was ready for him. She dug into the back pocket of her cut-offs, withdrew something obviously ripped from her journal, and handed it to him.

He looked at her inquiringly before unfolding the paper. "On the Beach," she'd written across the top. Joss swallowed, his heart clutched. He had trouble focusing on the poem. No, not poem: lyrics. *"We watch the sun sink slowly into the ocean/the yellows, the oranges, the fiery reds/fade into the pinks, blues and grays of dusk, fade into us. . . ."*

After a few lines he no longer saw just lyrics on a page, he heard them blend into the music—his music. He let the song play in his head; made a mental note that a bridge would have be written, where it would go.

"How badly does it suck?" Harper's voice jolted him back from creativity alley.

He put the song down, turned to her, and said what he knew he had to: "You're just like him, you know."

"Just like who?"

"Your father."

### Harper

Harper freaked. She jumped up off the sand and tried to run away, but Joss was quicker. He blocked her way, locked her in his arms. She didn't fight as hard as she could, wasn't even sure what the instinct to run was all about. Yet, there it was.

The song blaring from the housemates' CD player was "Love Shack," by the B-52's, and the others were dancing, Mitch, Mandy/Sarah, Katie, and Ali—shouting out the chorus: *"We can get to-ge-ther, love shack, baby! Woo!"*

Pulling away from Joss, Harper finally managed, "How long have you known?"

"If I tell you, promise not to run?"

The breeze that accompanied the just-beginning-to set sun toyed with his long hair. Harper resisted the urge to brush it out of his eyes. She let him lead her farther away from the group. Of all the annoying confessions, the things people "had to tell her" this last week, this was the least expected, the least welcome.

Joss began, "When I first met you, I was intrigued. There was something about you I couldn't pin. You reminded me of someone—the way you move, your expressions, the dimples—and even though I just came from touring with Jimi Jones, I didn't make the connection. Then we got to know each other, and when you told me you wrote poetry, when I realized it was more than that, there was music in your soul. You never said a word, and I respect your privacy—I probably would've let it go, kept it to myself."

"But?"

"I fell in love with you this summer."

Harper pretended not to hear that. She had enough to process.

"I don't want to hurt you," he said earnestly, reaching for her now. "It's just that I needed to know if you knew. And if you didn't, would it be okay if I told you? And if you did, is it okay that I know?"

Joss was rambling. When he rambled, his cool quotient plummeted below zero, so she reached for him—how could she not? "I know Jimi Jones is my father," she said, just above a whisper. "I've known since I was twelve."

"You do?" Joss looked surprised. "Do you want to meet him?"

Harper couldn't resist raising her eyebrows and quipping, "So, you can hook me up, huh?"

Joss was too far beyond the earnest-edge to go with the joke. He colored. "Harper, please understand. You are the coolest chick I've ever met. I've already screwed things up. We have something. I don't want to lose it."

She wanted to contradict him. They did not, in fact, "have something." They wouldn't be having a thing. It was, had to be, No thing. There were a million ways to say it, and she swore she was just about to. Instead, she heard herself ask, "What's he like?"

Finally, Joss smiled. God, he was cute when he smiled. "Jimi's really cool. For someone in his position—to his fans, he's like a rock god—he handles it amazingly well. He's still all about the music, a perfectionist. Somehow he's managed not to let the money, the power—the temptations—corrupt him. I've worked for other bands in the last few years, and he's by far the most real. He didn't know who I was, some anonymous roadie, but he always took the time to comment on my playing, to answer my questions—give advice, even."

"So are we nominating him for sainthood?" Harper muttered.

Josh laughed. "Sorry. People around him say he's mellowed over the years—if that means anything. Anyway, yesterday, I called him—to find out if he knew about you. Just so you know? He does, but all these years he's honored your mom's wishes to not intrude. If you say the word, he'll come."

She did not.

Joss said, "You know the song he ends every concert with? 'Under My Skin'? It was written for your mom. But you probably knew that."

Harper had suspected as much. Without realizing she was doing it, she sang softly, *"You were always the one/Your laugh, your eyes, your arms still/comfort me on rainy nights/You're under my skin/lady of my heart. . . ."*

He hadn't brought his guitar to the beach, so when Joss came in on harmony, it was a cappella. Harper, her own harshest critic, liked what she heard. Their voices wound around each other, blended, like that night on another beach. Only better.

Maybe Harper would meet Jimi Jones one day. With or without Joss's help. But never without her mom's knowledge, and her blessing. That, she could not, would not, do.

### *Mitch*

Mitch kicked back, out of breath. All the jogging he did, he was still panting from dancing, singing, and laughing. The relief of just letting go, not having to be anywhere, do anything, or prove anything to anyone: This was as fine a feeling as he'd ever had.

He surveyed the scene. What a mess! Empty shells, from the lobsters, crabs, mussels, and oysters, lay everywhere, punctuated by beer bottles, corncobs, scattered napkins, and used utensils.

No matter, there'd be plenty of time for cleaning up later.

Now was the time for chilling, his lady at his side, his friends close by, and his belly full. He leaned back on his elbows and stared out to the sea. The sun seemed to be balancing on the water's surface, like a perfect sphere, reminding him of that song his mother used to sing: *"And I think it's gonna be all right, Yeah, the worst is over now, the morning sun is shining like a red rubber ball."*

He thought of her now, long gone. And he suddenly knew how proud of him Dora Considine would be. Not because he'd achieved wealth or status, or had married—her expression—"some fancy, dancy" girl like Leonora, but because he'd escaped it. Long on the road from the prison of poverty to the lock-up of having to live by other people's standards, he'd found his own path. He could just be himself.

And that's all she'd really ever wanted.

Impulsively, he kissed Sarah's cheek. Causing her to turn just enough so their lips locked. Mmmm . . . lusty and luscious.

And so very unexpected.

Just like, he thought, grinning at his disparate housemates, the scraps. The scraps had really made it after all.

### Alefiya

Ali sat cross-legged on her blanket, Mitch and Sarah on one side, Katie on the other. She'd partaken of everything: from the thick, creamy clam chowder, lobster tail, two ears of corn; she'd even let Joss show her how to properly devour oysters, giggling as Harper merrily ragged on them both. Oysters might never be Harper's thing, but Ali could see now she'd have to teach Jeremy to enjoy them.

Jeremy! Her heart soared when she thought about him. She'd return to school in Boston next week, leaving Jeremy behind. Not for long, and surely not for good. She hadn't thought about finding a boyfriend this summer. That was a sweet, surprising bonus. She was seeing him later tonight, after the clambake, and they'd already made weekend plans to see each other in September.

She'd miss him until then, but needed time to work on her parents, anyway.

The *rumspringa*—to borrow that Amish phrase, since she still had none of her own—had turned out to be everything she'd hoped, and a whole lot more. She'd tasted freedom, found it sweet *and* bitter. The harshness of the scorn aimed at her after the robbery, the mistake of throwing the party, Mandy's taunts, and even Katie's thinly veiled contempt at the beginning of the summer, was hard. But on balance? It didn't come close to the joy she felt now. Alefiya would certainly return to her parents' world, honor their traditions. She loved them deeply, after all. But she would declare botany, not premed biology, as her major at school; she would be her own person. She would be with Jeremy.

"How're you doing?" It was Harper, who'd come to sit beside her now.

"Never better," Ali said. "The whole summer, the way everything turned out. I knew it'd be fun, but I didn't expect it to be this awesome. You . . . Joss . . . Mitch . . . even Sarah. Everyone's just exactly as they should be."

Harper put her arm around Ali, which started a chain reaction. Mitch and Sarah moved closer. Katie was squinched between Harper and Joss.

A snapshot from behind the group would show six friends sitting by the shoreline, close enough to touch, arms locked around each other's shoulders, silently watching the sun go down. Or, as Harper had poetically put it, watching the glorious array of yellows, oranges, and reds gradually fading into pinks, blues, and grays.

When it had just about set, Joss commanded, "Nobody move. I want to get something."

He returned not with a camera, but with six shot glasses, a bottle of tequila—the worm authenticated it—lime wedges, and a shaker of salt. Carefully, he divvied everything up, took his spot next to Katie, and instructed: "On my count. One . . ." Glasses were hoisted. "Two . . ." Chins tipped up. "Three!"

Down the hatch they went, first the salt, then the shot, and finally the lime-sucking ritual. The group's rhythm was off, but no one noticed. When the laughing, and coughing (Katie and Harper) died down, Mitch said it: "So, same time next year?"

## About the Author

RANDI REISFELD is the author of many, many best-selling media-based and original novels for teens and tweens, including three *New York Times* best-sellers. Her latest books, written with H. B. Gilmour, include the T*Witches series and *Oh Baby!*, published by Scholastic.

# ❀ WANTED ❀

## Single Teen Reader in search of a FUN romantic comedy read!

*How Not to Spend Your Senior Year*
BY CAMERON DOKEY

*Royally Jacked*
BY NIKI BURNHAM

*Ripped at the Seams*
BY NANCY KRULIK

*Cupidity*
BY CAROLINE GOODE

*Spin Control*
BY NIKI BURNHAM

*South Beach Sizzle*
BY SUZANNE WEYN & DIANA GONZALEZ

*She's Got the Beat*
BY NANCY KRULIK

*30 Guys in 30 Days*
BY MICOL OSTOW

Available from Simon Pulse ★ Published by Simon & Schuster

♥ ✿ ♥ ✿ ♥ ✿ ♥ ✿ ♥ ✿ ♥ ✿

# the party room

## by Morgan Burke

The party room is where all the prep school kids drink up and hook up. All you need is a fake ID and your best Juicy Couture to get in.

One night, Samantha Byrne leaves with some guy no one's ever seen before . . . and ends up dead in Central Park. Murdered gruesomely. Found at the scene of the crime: a school tie from Talcott Prep.

New York is suddenly in the grip of a raging media frenzy. And a serial killer walks amidst Manhattan's most privileged—and indulged—teens.

**From Simon Pulse**
Published by Simon & Schuster

"Nothing is more glam than a summer in the Hamptons." —*Teen Vogue*

"It's all too fabulous for words."—*Village Voice*

"Fans of the Gossip Girl series will love this novel." —*Teenreads.com*

# the au pairs

"A guilty-pleasure beach read!" —*Seventeen*

A NOVEL BY

## melissa de la cruz

"This is *Sex and the City* lite, where everyone is a little more fabulous, flirtatious, snobby, and deceitful than we are—and it's quite all right with us."—*Romantic Times Book Club*

"The ultimate summer."—*YM*

Published by
Simon & Schuster

Printed in the United States
By Bookmasters